The XYZ Affair

by Mary Billiter

© Copyright 2014 by Mary Billiter

978-1-940192-20-8

Published by
köehlerbooks ™

210 60th Street
Virginia Beach, VA 23451
212-574-7939
www.koehlerbooks.com

Publisher
John Köehler

Executive Editor
Joe Coccaro

DEDICATION

For the beautifully bald, blue-eyed newspaper editor who met me on Christmas so I wouldn't be alone. And then waited until I was ready for love. For the man who stole my heart by simply taking the lead. For the man who dances with me in the moonlight while Bob Dylan serenades us.

You are everything I ever dreamed and never imagined would happen. For my husband, Ron Gullberg, who showed me that lightening *does* strike twice and that happily ever after isn't just for fairy tales.

I will love you forever.

THE XYZ AFFAIR

A NOVEL

MARY BILLITER

VIRGINIA BEACH
CAPE CHARLES

CHAPTER 1

HOME. I didn't even know where that was anymore. I glanced at the GPS mounted on the windshield of my Suburban. By its calculations, I'd be at the only home whose doors hadn't closed on my children or me within ten to twenty minutes, depending on traffic.

Traffic on the two-lane highway had been thin until I had crossed county lines into Natrona, where more cars signaled to pass. It was Memorial Day weekend and everyone, it seemed, rushed to reach Wyoming's central city, Casper.

"Did you know a lot of the locals call it Ghost Town? *Get it?* Casper. Ghost." I glanced at my three children in the rearview mirror.

My teenager, Michael, rolled his eyes.

"Hey, check out the plane landing." I pointed out my side window.

The airport, tucked off the highway behind a canopy of aspen trees, waved their silvery leaves in the wind to welcome visitors to the Cowboy State.

We passed the airport just as quickly as I had announced it.

Casper's only a big city by Wyoming's standards; having more land than people. Most Wyomingites preferred it that way.

Two red bleeps on the GPS map signaled the turn off to my parent's house. I took a deep breath and stared at the green highway sign in the distance telling me to veer left. I knew the way to my parents' house, I just wasn't sure it was the way home.

I flipped on my turn signal and felt my heart keep rhythm with the constant clicking. *Oh God.* I hadn't eaten so I wasn't sure if the ache in my stomach was from hunger or dread.

I gripped the steering wheel. "Okay, we're getting close."

Michael's face popped up in the rearview mirror. The tension in my shoulders lessened as did my hold on the steering wheel. I smiled at him.

"So are Grandma and Grandpa excited that we're coming?" he asked.

I took another deep breath. "Excited?" I exhaled. "Upset is probably a bit more like it."

"They don't want us there?" Michael's teenage voice peeked and then dropped in octaves.

I glanced at him and lowered the volume on the car radio. One ear bud protruded from his ear and the other one dangled on his chest. His iPod leaned against his leg.

"Michael, Grandma and Grandpa are excited to see their grandbabies. They adore you. It's their forty-something-year-old daughter they aren't too thrilled with right now."

Michael sat back in his seat. I don't think he was too thrilled with me either. Uprooting my children from their fathers, friends and the Wyoming valley they had called home for more than a decade wasn't my first option. But when Cowboy State University called with a teaching job, I literally couldn't afford to pass it up.

I returned the rearview mirror to its original position and

wiped away the streaks of smeared mascara that circled my eyes. I looked like a raccoon and probably smelled like one too. *Lovely.*

With each passing street sign, my Suburban narrowed the distance between my parents and me. *Let this go well. Please.* My palms began to sweat. I quickly wiped them on my jeans and resumed steering.

"Yup, we're getting close."

Michael reached up and squeezed my shoulders. "Mom, relax." His hands had a tight massaging hold on my tense muscles. "It's only G-ma and G-pa."

"Okay, that's *our* nickname for them," I felt the tightness in my neck return, "but I don't think Grandpa would be too fond of it. So just call him Grandpa, okay? Or Professor Quinn; that'd really impress him."

"You gotta chill or you're going to have a heart attack."

I nodded. He was right. I looked forward and reacquainted myself with Casper.

"Oh hey," I wagged my finger. "Just up ahead is the square-shaped ice cream store." I turned right at the next intersection, but instead of seeing the corner store with ice cream cone decals dancing happily across the windows, I stared at an obnoxious neon green poster. "Coming Soon! Sam's Electronics."

"Ahh, man that stinks. It's the only place where you can get square-shaped ice cream in a square-shaped cone." I hit the steering wheel with the palm of my hand. "What the heck. We don't need an electronics store. We need our square-shaped ice cream."

Josie was laying her head on Izzy, our golden-mutt. Fred, her stuffed dog, was tucked between them. When Josie leaned forward to talk to me, Izzy groaned.

"Geez, Mom. It's *only* ice cream." Her long, chestnut hair

softly framed her face. Her brown eyes locked onto me in the rearview mirror. Josie and Michael were one of the few blessings from my first marriage. She squeezed my shoulder. "It's okay Mom, we'll find you another ice cream store. I promise. It'll be fun." Josie sat behind me so when she giggled it tickled my neck. I rubbed my shoulder against my ear.

"It won't be the same." I could hear the disappointment in my voice. "I was going to take you guys out for a cone later..." *When I needed a break from G-Ma and G-Pa.*

"I like ice cream, Momma." James tried to lean forward but the straps on his car seat secured him in place.

"Me too, buddy." I rapped my fingers against the steering wheel. My parents' house was less than a mile away.

"Okay, I *know* Hadley Field is just up ahead. I used to walk to it from G-ma's house." I turned around and quickly smiled at my three children. "It's where I learned to play soccer and ride a horse. I went to cheerleading camp there." I reached behind my seat and jostled Josie's knee. "Cheer camp is *so* much fun.

She mirrored her older brother and rolled her eyes.

I lowered my speed and slowly drove past the field. The fence was still there, but monuments and tombstones rose from the ground in a perfect lined formation. A white cross was attached to the entry gate.

"Oh, no." My voice sank along with my spirits. "It's a cemetery."

"Oh snap!" Michael started laughing. "It looks like everything you love is dead, gone or buried."

"Not funny. I loved Hadley Fields. It was a great, safe place to hang out when I was your age." I slapped my thigh. "Did you know I learned to roller skate there?"

"Wow. That's really lame," Michael said with a grin.

I chuckled. "No, it was so much fun. I had my own pair of

skates and I wore my rainbow striped terry cloth tank top and white dolphin shorts..." *That showed off half my ass to your father.* "It was great." I stared longingly at the field of rich green grass that was marred by death. *I had my first kiss there.*

Thoroughbred Estates was straight ahead. I waited at the stop sign and looked at the gated community. I blew out a mouthful of air. *Great.*

It sure wasn't the old neighborhood. If it were, our two-story house would have had its summer coat of paint and my big red, 1997 Suburban would have fit in perfectly. But as my father, the professor, gained stature at the University, so did our housing.

I didn't bother to look either way as I drove through the last intersection. My car dipped up and over the speed bump that signaled the entrance into my parents' subdivision. The guard stopped me at the gate and handed me a map with streets that were named to match the equestrian motif.

My parents' home was on Bridle. Their house was an "L"-shaped, two-story, wood-sided structure. I would have said it was typical of Wyoming, but it wasn't. The architect had taken curves out of the equation and replaced them with sharp edges and hard angles. The large flat facets and mammoth size made it more futuristic than rustic.

"That's their new house?" Michael asked.

"Weird, huh?" I said. "I've only been in it once and it was, well...odd."

Josie rubbed her eyes and yawned. "It's different."

I leaned forward and peered at it through the windshield. The only Wyoming element that remained was that it was built on the bank of the North Platte River. The neighboring lots were ten acres each with a mandatory one-acre setback.

"It's different *and* expensive. G-ma told me they had to pay more money for their lot and they couldn't build close to the river."

"Why?" Josie asked.

"To preserve the river views for the residents who weren't *lucky* enough to have their custom home built on a bluff that faces the Platte."

"Oh." Josie leaned her head back.

I gazed at my parents' house. It was Shangri-La in a rugged Western town. The dual combination of mountain views and river frontage, though, was hard to argue. My father's new car, on the other hand, wasn't.

"Son of a bit..." I stopped short. *He couldn't buy a magazine subscription for Josie's school fundraiser, but...* A 2012 silver Beemer coupe was parked behind my mom's covered car. *Must be nice.*

I cut the engine and stared at the personalized plate on the back. As the largest county in Wyoming, Natrona was ranked first. License plates began with the county seat followed by a silhouette of a bucking horse and rider and then the license number or in my Dad's case, vanity message. From a distance it read #1 PROF. *Oh, brother.*

"Is that G-pa's car?" Michael gripped the back of the front seat. My body pulled toward him. "No, way. That is so sick."

I couldn't respond. I looked at the car whose worth alone could cover my living expenses for a year.

My mom suddenly opened the front door to her house. I turned in her direction.

Michael quickly unbuckled James from his car seat and the kids rushed to meet her. She hugged and kissed each of them before they ran into the house.

Okay...here I go.

I stepped out of the Suburban. My mom was thinner, but when she slightly tilted her head I heard the words that weren't being spoken. *Are you alright?*

I shook my head.

She waved me toward her.

Her perfume held me before she did. She opened her arms. I walked into them.

"Oh, Dani." She kissed the side of my head. "You're home."

I felt my eyes well up and a year's worth of hurt run down my face. *Mom.* I couldn't speak. The knot in my throat prevented words from coming forward and pain from being swallowed.

"I've been so worried about you."

My chest rattled.

She held me tightly. "Shh," she said, "It's okay."

Josie ran out of the house and wrapped her arms around my waist. "Ahh, Mom, don't cry."

I quickly wiped my eyes and pinched the snot from my nose, wiping it on my jeans. "Oh, baby girl, I'm okay. It's just...I haven't seen my mom in a long time."

Mom gently patted the top of Josie's head. "Now, we'll see each other all the time."

I looked into the house. "Where's Dad?"

"Oh, your father's been napping so he might be a bit groggy and distant."

I checked my watch. "The Professor napping?" I rolled my eyes. "I don't think so."

"No, he does rest from time to time."

"Sure. Dad never rests..." *And God help any of his children who do. Rest.* It wasn't in his vocabulary. *Now, hiding to avoid something or someone...that's more like him.*

"Five years." His voice reached the front porch.

I watched my father. His steps were measured with precision. He approached the entry hall of his house the way he walked in a college commencement ceremony. Joe Quinn did not believe in anything less than perfection.

He stood stoically in front of me. I have described my father as thin, but never gaunt. His face had lost any fullness it had. I stopped myself from gasping.

"Hi, Dad."

"Five years," he repeated.

I held my hands palm up like they were scales and slightly moved them up and down, weighing what to say. "Five years?"

"Since you've been home."

"Oh." I clenched my jaw. *And here we go.*

"Five years," he said.

I nodded. *How 'bout we make it another five and I leave? I'm sure there's still a hotel in town that hasn't converted into something else.*

He stiffly held out his arms. "Daniella."

It sounded more like a question than a request.

I went to him. His arms perfunctorily patted my back. I'm sure Frankenstein embraced people the same way.

When he released me he looked at my kids. "Three children." His head bounced as he glanced at each one.

"Yes, Dad, you remember...Michael, Josie and James."

A flicker of life sparked in his eyes when his gaze landed on James.

I bit my lip. James, my only child from my second marriage, had his father's stocky build, but my strong dark Irish features.

My father lightly tapped the end of James' nose. "Aren't you a handsome boy?"

"Yes, I am." James stood with pride before my Dad.

I laughingly smiled.

Michael scooped James up and kissed his neck. James giggled. Michael set him back down. "Hey buddy. Are you going to show G-..." Michael grinned at me, *"Grandpa* how to fish?"

"That would be grand," my dad said. He bent down toward James. "Did your dad teach you how to fish?"

"Chase didn't, I did," Michael stepped toward his little brother. "I took James fishing."

I swallowed, but the lump had returned. *That's not Michael's job. His father should have taught him.* My dad was probably thinking the same thing.

Now, he turned his attention toward my suitcase-stuffed Suburban. "It looks like you packed to stay a while."

Michael shot me a quizzical look.

"Uh, yeah...Dad, we're moving to Casper."

"That's right." He slowly nodded. "That's right." He lightly massaged his neck. "It is a shame you had to leave such a beautiful valley and home."

No, it's a shame that Chase couldn't be faithful and then to top it off decided he didn't want a family.

"I suppose it reinforces the truth about statistics." My father made eye contact with me. "Sixty percent of second marriages end in divorce."

Wow. His comment pierced through me. I refused to yield to the pain. I smiled in his direction. *Thank you, Professor, for that statistical lesson on the shambles of my life.* My lip began to quiver. I bit it down. *Where would I be if I didn't have him to remind me of my failings?*

"Can I get Izzy?" Josie looked up at me.

"Uh, actually," my mom said. "I'd rather not have dog hair in the house."

Josie sniffled and her voice cracked. "You're not going to leave Izzy out in the car, are you? What are we going to do with her?"

"Well," my mom said. "There's the barn or the garage."

"Uhh..." I pursed my lips.

My mom patted me on the back. "I'll let you work this out with your children." She walked into the house. Dad followed.

I curtly smiled at their backs. "Thanks."

All three children stared at me.

"It's cold and it's been raining. She can't stay outside. It's not warm enough yet." Michael served as the spokesman for the clan.

"Okay." I held up my hand. "Let me think."

Josie handed me my cell phone that was tucked beside Fred, her stuffed dog, in the crook of her arm. "It beeped that it was fully charged."

I scrolled through the contacts. "Oh, hey. I could call Ruth. She's the secretary at the college that's been helping me with all my new-hire paperwork. I could see if we could leave Izzy with her. She said she lives close to Grandma."

"Does she like dogs?"

I shrugged. "Doesn't everyone in Wyoming?"

"Except G-ma and G-pa," Michael said.

"Shh!" I huddled my children around me and whispered. "They summer in Wyoming and winter in California. They don't have time for a dog. It's different. Don't worry I'll make sure Izzy's okay and that she's somewhere warm." *And trust me kids, there's not a lot of warmth where we're staying.*

I called Ruth's cell phone and within minutes her address was plugged into the GPS.

My mom's spotless entry way donned a row of shoes lined up beside the front door. Her house rule dictated that all shoes come off before entering. If I pulled off my boots, it was going to be for the night.

Ah, the hell with it. "Mom!" I yelled into the house. "I'm taking the kids with me. We're going to drop off Izzy."

Mom walked from the kitchen with a spatula in her hands.

"I'll put your dinner in the oven. It's important that your father eat at six. We won't be able to wait."

"Okay...sorry?" *Geez. Naps in the afternoon. Dinner at six. I seriously need to retire.*

CHAPTER 2

A DAY of intermittent rain had cleared the Wyoming sky. A cloudless evening stretched before us when we returned to my parent's gated community. Their house wasn't lit.

"Let me go first. Maybe Grandma turned off the lights to save on electricity." I turned around in the Suburban. "Don't leave. I'll be right back."

I found a note taped to the front door.

Dani –

Your father and I had to attend a library meeting. We tried to reach you on your cell phone, but there was no answer. We didn't want to leave the key under the doormat. We thought you'd be here sooner. See you in a little bit.

Love,

Mom

"You're kidding." I ripped the paper off the door. "You don't want to leave a key under the mat? This is Wyoming. People leave their car keys in the ignition." I stomped my foot on their wood deck. "Son of a—"

"You must be Helen's daughter, Dani?"

I jumped. "Damn it!"

"I'm sorry. I didn't mean to startle you." A man close to six feet tall with a stocky, broad-shouldered, football player build approached the porch and I backed away in equal measure.

"Who are you? What do you want?" I reached into the back pocket of my jeans. It was empty. My cell phone was in the car. *Shit. Shit. Shit.*

The man stopped on the bottom step leading to the porch and removed his cowboy hat. "I'm Chris Gorham." He pointed his lid toward the shadows that had crept on my parents' lawn. "I live next door. Well, actually, in the next lot." He lightly chuckled, "It's not quite next door."

I slowly nodded. "And you're here because..."

"Oh, of course." He put his boot on the next stair and stepped into the light from my Suburban's high beams. The sleeves of his denim shirt were caked in dry mud and his jeans weren't any better looking. His black cowboy boots were dust-covered.

Wonderful. Another cowboy. Just what I need.

"Your parents gave me their spare house key and left a message that you might be driving in soon." He reached into his jeans front pocket. "If there's anything I can do..." His head was shaved with a hint of dark stubble that oddly made me want to rub my hand across it to feel the grizzled hair move back and forth.

He handed me a key ring in the shape of the letter "O." A fighting duck holding a football was in the center of the green symbol. "It's the middle key. The other two are for the garage and barn."

"Thank you." I turned toward my parents' front door.

"The lock's a little tricky. If you'd like me to..." He took a step toward the last stair.

"Listen." I spun around and found myself face-to-face with

him. His eyes were the color of sapphire that I'd only seen on the flat-sided gin bottles behind the bar when I waitressed. His eyes were beautiful and his glassy sapphires were staring back at me. "Um, Mr. Gorham, is it?"

"Or Gorm."

I clenched my jaw. "Well, *Gorm,* I've been up since five this morning packing and cleaning my rental with the slim possibility I'll get my deposit returned. I've had three kids, a dog and all the Country Western music I want to hear for a decade going nonstop in the car for six, no correction, *seven* hours. I'm tired, I stink and I'm hungry. I don't need any more cowboys or anyone else trying to rescue me. Thank you for the keys, but I've got it from here."

His mouth formed the same *O* on his key ring. "Ohhh-kay, then." He pivoted to leave.

I massaged my temple. "Gorm."

With his hat in his hand, he glanced up from the bottom step.

"I'm sorry. Thanks for coming over. Really. I didn't mean to be a jerk."

He slowly nodded. "Sure. Welcome to Casper." Then he made his way into the darkness.

Great. You just managed to tick off the neighbor and probably the only guy in this freaking community that's under the age of sixty. Swell.

After Gorm's warning, I expected a fight with the front lock. The door, though, opened effortlessly. *Finally. Something that works.* I palmed the wall for the light switch panel. I flipped them all and found yet another note on the entry hall table.

Dani –

Hopefully you've met Chris. A lovely young man. (And single too.) Dinner's in the oven – there's enough to share if you'd like to invite Chris. Please clean up your mess. See you soon.

Love,

Mom

I threw my hands up in the air and hit the note on the table. It fell to the floor like a lead zeppelin. "Really, Mom? Single. Dinner invite. I don't know where to begin."

"Is G-ma being a bi-atch?"

"Michael!" I whirled around. Michael's cheeks were red and he was smiling.

"Sorry, Mom. It just seems like G-ma's being a real d-bag."

I knew I should have been shocked by my son's language, but I wasn't. Instead of gasping, a high-pitch giggle escaped. It sounded like helium leaving a balloon.

"What the hell? Was that a laugh or a cry?"

I chuckled and again it sounded like a cartoon character. "Oh, geez." I giggled deliriously. "I'm losing it. I need sleep." I took a deep breath and exhaled. My cheeks hurt from smiling.

"Michael," I pointed my index finger at him and tried to sound authoritarian. "Watch your mouth. G-ma's being a little bit of a pill, but I love her and we are her guests."

"Guests? We're her family." Josie walked into the house. James pulled up the rear.

"Hey!" I clapped my hands together in a weak attempt to rally my troops and switch the topic. "Let's unload the car and then eat. I'm starving." I poked Josie in the belly and made her smile. "Maybe afterward we can go find a new ice cream shop."

Within an hour of dropping Izzy off and unloading our luggage, I received a frantic call from Ruth saying that Izzy escaped. I quickly reloaded the kids into the Suburban. I pulled out of my parents' front drive when I saw the soft yellow lights from the oversized front windows of the neighboring house. *Why is it so difficult to ask for help?* I drummed my fingers against the steering wheel and slowly drove forward. *Worse thing he could say is 'no' and it's not like I haven't heard that before?* "Oh, what the hell."

I drove toward his house and pulled into the circular drive. His house reminded me of something I'd seen featured in a Wyoming homes magazine.

"Wow. This is nice." Josie's voice perked up.

The log construction had an elegant lodge-type feel with a massive stone fireplace that inched up the side of the house. The wood detail and large trusses in the grand cathedral entrance revealed the natural richness of Wyoming. The porch light beckoned me forward. I ran to the entryway and knocked on the double oak doors. I tapped my foot on the front porch. The wood flooring created an echo. I tapped until Gorm opened the front door.

He stood in the threshold. "Is everything okay?"

"Actually, our dog, Izzy, ran away."

"Well, she couldn't have gone far. The community's gated."

I scuffed the tip of my boot on his welcome mat. "I kind of left her with a colleague."

"Oh."

I glanced up. His blue eyes locked onto me. "I know. I screwed up. Is there any way you could go with us?" I wanted to close my eyes, thinking it might drown out the sound of him rejecting me. Instead, I pleaded my case. "I *used* to know Casper, but it's changed...hell, I don't know it at all. I don't even know where to look."

There it was. Nothing more to say. He could either slam the door and walk away, which after the way I snapped at him earlier, I really wouldn't blame him. Or...

"Let me grab a flashlight."

I let out a sigh. Relief instantly flooded my body. Tension started to work its way out of my bundled nerves.

Gorm disappeared into his house. Yet when he returned so did my defenses. He had a flashlight and a beanie. He slid the wool cap over his head. "My head gets cold even in the summer."

"What about your cowboy hat?" The words and cynicism escaped my mouth before I could take them back.

Gorm touched his chin and started to brush the shadow of a beard. "I was covering the rodeo tonight."

"Covering the rodeo?" The tone of my voice was sharp and edgy.

"I'm a sports writer. When you cover a college or national rodeo, you don't show up in a suit."

I glanced at the wood flooring.

"Other than the occasional rodeo assignment," his voice was unwaveringly firm; "I only wear my lid when I'm out in the sun to protect my head from burning. Or when I'm at my Mom's ranch, helping her out. Otherwise, it's my Oregon beanie."

I looked up at him and felt the heat of humiliation creep into my cheeks. "I'm sorry. That was so rude. It's none of my business what you wear." I pressed my thumb against the side of my head and pushed against the throbbing tension. "I don't know what's gotten into me. I'm really grateful you're willing to help."

He smiled. "Glad to."

Why is he so nice? Be a jerk. I know how to handle that.

Gorm suggested Michael stay at my parents' house with James and that he'd drive. No one argued. Josie and I piled into his green Jeep and strapped in. Gorm phoned in a pizza order before we pulled out of the gated community.

"Let the boys know that Mario's Pizza will be bringing by the house special. It's paid for. All they have to do is open the door.

Mario's has been approved by the community board and so have his drivers. He's safe. And the food is delicious."

"Wow. Okay. Thanks. My mom made dinner, but it looked pretty..." I cringed. "Well, it looked awful."

Gorm chuckled. It was low, raspy and oddly, incredibly sexy.

"Thanks for doing that. You didn't need to."

"I know. I wanted to." He looked my way. "Now I don't have to bring over a welcome plate of cookies."

I smiled and reached into my back jean pocket and felt for my phone. "Damn it." I let out a loud breath. "I left my phone on the hall table."

Gorm handed me his iPhone. I texted Michael. Gorm's phone beeped seconds later. I held the phone out to read the text.

"*K. Bnice. Dude-s GR8. LOL.*" The returned text, when deciphered, read: *Okay. Be nice. Dude's great. Laugh out loud.* The LOL had become Michael's signature tag to every text as if everything he texted was funny and he was literally laughing out loud as he sent it.

My fingers pressed firmly into the alphabet keypad on Gorm's phone. *"Don't care if the dude is great. Not interested—ever. Open the door for Mario and make sure James gets something to eat. LOL."*

I placed Gorm's phone in the car's cup holder. He handed me two white pills.

"What's this?"

"Aspirin. It looked like you could use some."

"Oh. Thanks."

He extended a bottle of water.

"Wow. You've got everything." *Did I seriously just gush over two aspirin? Really. Why am I letting this guy get to me? It's only aspirin.*

"Uh..." Gorm slightly hesitated. "It's nothing." His voice had a hint of self-consciousness. "Just the essentials. It's really no big deal."

When he hit the window control, the Wyoming wind swept into the Jeep and drowned out any chance of him hearing me make any more stupid remarks. A light rain added to my relief when it sprinkled my reddened face. Josie and I called for our dog.

"Izzy! Izzy! Here girl."

In the dark, I felt as lost in Casper as Izzy.

I pressed the button to roll up my window. I stopped halfway. "Where would she go?" I mumbled.

"Somewhere open," Gorm said. "From what your mom told me she's a country dog."

"I'm sure my mom said she was like Cujo, too."

Gorm glanced at me. "She didn't say anything like that, but nice Stephen King reference."

For some reason a big smile filled my face.

We circled Ruth's neighborhood multiple times with no sign of my dog.

"Mom, she's used to open fields," Josie said.

Josie's reasoning brought me back to center. "Baby girl, I have no idea where that would be."

"I do." Gorm pointed toward a street. "It's Wyoming Boulevard. It wraps around the city and there are fields on either side. Ruth's neighborhood backs up to it."

He drove and Josie and I called for Izzy.

Gorm pulled into an open lot.

"This is Cheney High School."

A battleground of behemoth machinery sat vacant along the southwest corner of the parking lot, the claw of the excavator poised in the air like a ravaging dinosaur. A snaking orange security fence that wrapped around the construction site surrounded huge mounds of dirt. A sentinel of silver spotlights guarded the plot. *Under Construction, Cheney High Athletic Field* a large white sign announced. The wide stretch of land suited a country dog like Izzy.

We yelled until her name was barely audible from our scratched throats. I massaged my neck while Gorm started to pull out of the lot. Josie pointed to a dark silhouette in the distance.

"There she is!"

The Jeep continued to putter forward.

"Stop!" I fumbled to unlock the doors, but the child safety locks were activated. "Unlock the damn doors!"

Gorm pushed a button on the side of his car door releasing the locks. By the time he stopped and we got out, Izzy had once again run off into the shadows.

"You've got to learn to stop on a freaking dime!" I glared at Gorm. "Lightning *doesn't* strike twice."

He steadied me with intense steel blue eyes. "Sometimes, Dani, it does."

I held his gaze for a moment and then looked away. "Whatever. Just drive me home."

"Gladly."

The clock in my father's study chimed at midnight when Gorm dropped Josie and me off at my parents', who were asleep; but Michael had waited up. He gave me the same hard stare I gave Gorm when we walked in without Izzy.

"I'm sorry. We'll find her. I promise."

"You're kidding me, right?" Michael slammed the palm of his hand on the kitchen counter.

I jumped.

"That's great, Mom. Just super. We're here like, what an hour, and you've already managed to run off another member of our family."

I lowered my head. Tears welled in the corners of my eyes. "I'm sorry. I'm so sorry."

"You are sorry. You're a sorry excuse for a parent. I wish I had stayed with Dad. At least then I wouldn't have to deal with another one of your train wrecks."

"Michael, that's not fair." Josie's eyes brimmed with tears. "It's not Mom's fault. She didn't lose Izzy."

"Nooo. You're right, Josie, it's never Mom's fault. She's just a victim of circumstance." Michael shot me a glare. His hazel eyes were an angry shade of green. "Isn't that right, *Mom*? Isn't that how you explained it to everyone in town?"

"Go to hell." I walked toward the stairs.

Michael called out after me. "I'm already in it."

Josie followed behind me. Her eyes were puffy from crying. She was asleep within minutes of hitting the pillow on the bed we shared in the upstairs guest room. I lay beside her exhausted, but my mind wouldn't rest. Izzy always laid on my feet.

"I don't know what I'm supposed to do." I spoke to the ceiling. "It's a mess." I bit the inside of my cheek but it didn't stop me from crying. "Michael's right. I'm a train wreck."

I rolled my head back and forth on the pillow. "Please bring her back. Please." The pillow was wet from collecting the heartache that poured out of me. "We can't have another member of our family leave us. Not now. They don't deserve that. My kids don't deserve this."

I slumped out of bed and folded onto my knees. I hadn't prayed in a long time and now it seemed like a *Hail Mary* was in order.

"Please. I can't lose her. Not now. Please. Just bring her back. She's my dog. She's loyal. She's sweet. She's mine. I'm sorry. Michael will never forgive me. Please. I can't lose my son and my dog. Please just bring her back."

The next morning we rose early to the doorbell's chime. Gorm stood on the front porch. He wore a green University of Oregon hoodie and jeans that weren't splattered with mud. Donald Duck was centered against the *O* on his chest.

His hands were outstretched with a box of bagels, tubs of assorted cream cheese, and a carton of orange juice balanced in one hand and a cup of coffee in the other.

"Why are you here?" I asked. *I was such a bitch to you.*

"I've got nothing better to do." He shrugged with a grin.

I chuckled. "You're serious." *Damn the cowboy code and the cute men who uphold it.*

He flashed a crooked smile, offering a warm cup of coffee.

"I wasn't sure how you take it. There's cream and sugar in the cup holder of my car. I figured after the day you had yesterday you could use it. And if you don't, I will."

Gorm shifted his attention to Michael. "If you don't mind waiting here again with your little brother, I'd like to take your mom and sister back out to look for Izzy. I'm sure we'll find her."

Gorm reached out and gently touched my arm. "I know how important she is to you."

I raised my shoulders and felt my throat constrict. "She's my Smith and Wesson."

Gorm scratched his bald head.

"She has the innate ability to alert me...stranger danger and all. I don't need a gun when Izzy's around. She's the best protection I have."

"Then we're going to bring her back. Wyoming's pretty serious about our right to bear arms and we're even more serious when those arms are threatened."

I smiled. "Good to know."

Gorm headed toward his Jeep.

"I'll be right there," I called out.

I cozied up beside Michael in the kitchen. He was leaning over the counter tearing a chunk of bagel off with his metal-covered teeth. "Are you okay if I go back out with Josie?" He wouldn't look at me. "Michael?"

His face tightened and he spoke to the counter. "Fine. Do what you got to do. I'll spend my summer watching James."

"It's not like that. I don't want to ask my parents' yet...I'm sorry. Once we get Izzy back, I promise we'll get back on track. And you have football camp in a few days."

Michael cocked his head toward me. I felt my stomach drop. *He's leaving me too.* I bit down hard on the inside of my cheek. He couldn't see me break down.

"Mom." He placed his hand on my shoulder. I tightened beneath his touch. He softened his hold. "It's okay. I'm just..."

"No, it's not okay, but I'm going to make it better. I promise."

"Mom! Gorm's in the Jeep. Are you coming?" Josie yelled from the doorway.

"Go." Michael pushed me forward. "I'm okay. I got this. Go get Izzy."

I sat in the passenger's seat beside Gorm and stared vacantly out of the side window. "He'll never forgive me if I lose Izzy."

Gorm slid a CD into the Jeep's stereo and adjusted the volume so the speakers resonated in the back where Josie was sitting. He leaned toward the center console. "He's what, fifteen or sixteen?"

"Fifteen." I moved toward him.

"He's got a lot more going on than just a lost dog. Fifteen's a tough age. He's not quite a man, but he's no longer a boy."

I stared at Gorm. His Roman nose was solid and distinctive. *Greek or Jewish? Does it even matter?*

"My sons are older now, but I remember."

I watched him. When Gorm spoke it exaggerated his strong, defined jawline and created a powerful profile. *Whatever he is... it's hot.*

"The teenage years weren't easy," he said.

"How many sons do you have?"

Gorm glanced in his rearview mirror and switched lanes. "Two boys. My youngest just moved out."

"Oh, geez. You're married." I slapped my chest with my hand. *I'm going to hell.* "I'm so sorry. Your wife must think I'm awful for taking up all your time."

"Not likely," he laughed. "My ex is somewhere in the Bahamas with her latest boy toy. No chance of her worrying about anything."

"Huh." I slightly looked up toward the ceiling of the Jeep. *Thank you, God.* It's the first time I ever thanked the heavens for someone's divorce.

"What?" Gorm leaned forward to look out the passenger side mirror. The fragrance of fresh unwrapped soap combined with the spicy scent of his deodorant was an intoxicating cocktail for the senses. I drew a deep breath. He gave me a sideways glance.

"Oh." *Just smelling your hotness.* I returned my focus to the alley we had just entered. "I never thought you were married or divorced." *But divorced is good.*

Gorm slowed down the speed of his Jeep. "It's tough to be the new one in town..." His voice trailed off.

Oh great. Here comes the "things will look brighter tomorrow" speech. I'm sure I've got my mom to thank for this little pep talk. I'm sure she told the neighbor all about her pathetic daughter. Wonderful.

"But Dani," Gorm boldly reached over and gently touched my knee. "You're not the only one who's gone through this."

Huh. I looked at his hand and then at him. He didn't

withdraw his hand or his eye contact. *Didn't see that coming.*

"Gorm, you're right, but this isn't my first rodeo."

He nodded. I couldn't help staring into his eyes. *They're amazing.*

"Then you know how rodeos work. Sometimes," he said and then tightened his grip on my knee, "you just need to hold on for eight seconds."

I wanted to reach down and grab his hand. I wanted the life vest he was throwing me, but my chest deflated with air. "I'm trying." I looked at him. "It's not always that easy. And it sure doesn't help that this is my second one."

Gorm bobbed his head. "Well," he casually withdrew his hand from my knee and a slow smile spread across his face, "I'm a sports writer."

I found myself smiling along with him. "Yeah..."

"And if I've learned one thing over the years, Dani, it's that it takes *three strikes* before you're out."

I started to laugh.

"From where I'm sitting," the tone of his voice, like his smile, was infectious, "you've still got one more crack at the plate."

I threw my head back and laughed for the first time in the last twenty-four hours.

Gorm continued to drive down back roads, alleys and past parks. There wasn't any sign of my gold mutt. I checked my watch.

"In five minutes I have a scheduled realtor appointment."

I glanced over my shoulder at Josie to pat her knee when I spotted my weathered Smith & Wesson.

"Stop!"

Gorm slammed on the brakes and hit the side remote to unlock the doors. I fumbled my way out of my seatbelt. I bolted down the street toward my dog.

I never thought I was a dog person until I met Izzy three years ago. She was a puppy in a box outside a grocery store. I instantly knew she belonged to me. So when she jumped into my arms and pushed me onto the pavement, the acrid scent of wet dog never smelled so good. I honestly couldn't tell who cried harder, Izzy or me. She was back. *We haven't lost her. Michael. She came back.*

Josie ran to us and wrapped her arms around Izzy and me.

Gorm stood above me. His eyes matched the clear blue Wyoming sky.

"Sometimes, Dani," he said and lightly kicked my shoe with his boot, "lightning does strike twice."

CHAPTER 3

"DANI, YOU'VE got mail."

I rolled my eyes. "Mom, that's not possible. I just put in my change of address card."

"Well, it has your name on it."

I grabbed the envelope. Dani Quinn.

I opened it to find an American Association of Retired Persons card with my name imprinted on it.

"What?" *This has got to be a mistake.* I scanned the AARP letter. The nonprofit, nonpartisan organization's goal was to help people fifty and over improve the quality of their lives. My AARP card was one phone call away from activation which would allow me to start "embracing the perks, and quirks, of getting older."

"But I'm only forty-four." *And living back at my parent's house: isn't that enough humiliation?*

Mom looked over my shoulder. "Oh, the AARP. They have such good benefits. Your father and I get into the movies for half the cost of a regular ticket."

It's not that my budget couldn't use the extra discount, but I'm not ready to embrace the perks and quirks of getting older.

Or be the third wheel on my parent's date.

"Maybe when I'm closer to fifty or sixty I'll activate my membership, but I've still got six good years ahead of me."

My mother wiped her hands on the dishtowel draped over her shoulder. "Dani Maureen, no one's saying your old."

"I know! *I* didn't even say I was old. Why would you even bring that word up?"

Mom pursed her lips.

"What?" I asked.

"I saw your eye cream in the guest bathroom."

I shrugged. "So? It's for my eyes. They get puffy."

Mom turned my cheek toward her. "Dani, you've been through a lot this last year."

I glanced at the hardwood floors in her hallway. "I know and it shows under my eyes. I never had these wrinkles before."

She tilted my chin up. "My Swedish grandmother called them crow's feet, but I always thought that sounded awful. Your grandmother, my mother, said the fine lines under or around our eyes show wisdom..."

"Then Slim's one wise woman."

Mom and I turned in the direction of the front door. My younger brother, Finnegan or "Finn" as we called him, stood in the entryway.

I smiled at the sibling I most resembled. Finn and I could have been fraternal twins. We both had the same matching brown eyes and chocolate brown hair, although mine had blonde highlights. While we looked like each other, Finn often reminded me that my eyes were darker. "Black as coal," he said, "like your soul." We resembled the dark Irish side of my father's family.

My older sister, Fiona, and older brother, Sean, looked like my mom. Swedes. Blondes with blue eyes. It was a startling contrast when all of us got together for a family photo.

My thirty-nine-year-old baby brother smiled as he took off his raincoat and hung it on the horseshoe hook mounted on the wall.

"So forty isn't the new twenty?" He walked toward me and snapped his fingers. "Damn." Finn was approaching his fortieth birthday in a few short months.

I chuckled. "Apparently not, brother. Forty-something is closer to fifty and the new retirement age."

"I have a better chance of that happening than you do, lil' Slim."

"Thanks for the vote of confidence."

"Why does Uncle Finn call you, 'Slim'?"

James sat on the staircase leaning his head on one of the slots in the wooden banister. Finn stepped toward him, reached his hand through the railing and gently tapped James on the nose.

"I call your momma 'Slim' because there was a time in her life when she wasn't."

James giggled. "Momma, you were fat?"

"I ate to escape life when I was living with your uncle."

Finn tilted his head toward me. "I wasn't the one selling Girl Scout cookies and eating all the inventory."

I smiled when really I shouldn't have because it'd only add more wrinkles. "Thanks. I'm already a hard critic of myself since I hit the forty mark. This recruitment brochure," I swatted Finn with the letter, "isn't helping my age-esteem issues, and neither are you."

"So it'd bother you if I said you had more crow's feet than a Kansas corn field?"

His deadpan delivery made me laugh despite myself.

"Finnegan, now you stop it," Mom said. "Dani's a beautiful

woman in the prime of her life. She'll find someone who'll appreciate her wisdom."

"Great." I kneaded my forehead.

"Mom, I agree. He'll have to be blind, but it's possible. Dani hasn't dated this side of the state yet."

"Really? I haven't *dated* anyone in six years. The last date I went on ended in a marriage proposal...and we all know how well that turned out for me."

"Oh, Dani." My mom walked to the staircase. "I'm glad you met your cowboy. We wouldn't have James Patrick if you hadn't."

I swallowed the lump in my throat. *I didn't mean to hurt him.* "I loved my cowboy, Mom. And..." I quickly raced up the stairs to where James sat. "I love, love, love my little cowboy." I squeezed him. *Please forgive my big mouth and me.* His blonde hair smelled like baby shampoo. *Don't grow up. Don't ever grow up.*

"James Patrick Arnold!" he shouted.

"That's right." Pride filled my face. "In preschool, they taught him how to spell his name. James wanted to know how to spell his *whole* name."

"That's my boy." Finn held up his hand, "Gimme five."

James slapped it through the stair slats.

"So where's the other rug rats?" Finn scanned the front of the house.

"They're all in the basement watching some hunting show with Dad."

"How have things been between you two?" Finn asked.

I stood and brushed dog hair off my blouse. After Izzy went missing, I told Mom she wasn't going to go anywhere we weren't. "So what's the plan for today?"

"I guess that answers my question."

I raised my index finger. "One disaster at a time."

Finn clapped his hands. "Okay then. Melissa and the kids are waiting for me at the hotel. I thought I'd take your bunch into town with us for some shopping and possibly bowling."

I softly smiled. "Thanks, Finn. How long are you guys here?"

"I lucked out. My meetings wrapped up on Friday so I was able to tack on the holiday weekend *and* the rest of the week."

"Finnegan flies back to California on Friday." Mom wrapped her arm around my little brother who stood a foot taller than both of us. Finn kissed the top of her head.

"Ah," I said with a delightful tone to my voice. "June first, same day I begin teaching summer school."

Finn smiled. "I'm really proud of you for getting this job."

I glanced at my watch. "Shit. I'm supposed to be at the college for registration. *Crap!* I already missed my appointment with the realtor. I can't miss this." I spotted my briefcase on the entry hall table. "Okay." I pointed my finger at my mom and then brother. "You got this covered, right?"

They nodded.

"I don't know how long I'll be. Ruth told me they were setting up a book signing so students and the community could come meet me."

James ran down the stairs and jumped into my arms. "Have a good day at work."

I closed my eyes and held him. His heart beat rapidly against my chest. "I'm going to miss you, baby."

James wiggled out of my arms. Finn tousled his hair. "We're going to have fun. Tell your mom to stop worrying."

James swatted me on the backside. "Go get 'em, Momma!"

I left to begin my new job with a smile and more hope than I had felt in a while. *Maybe, just maybe, this time it'll all work out.*

CHAPTER 4

AN ORANGE, triangular-shaped sign stood in the middle of the three-way intersection at Cowboy State University.

Road Work Ahead in black letters glistened in the morning light. I tilted my Suburban's sun visor to block the glare. In all three directions cranes, excavators and mustard-yellow colored backhoes moved and pushed dirt, hoisting steel beams in the air or clawing at the ground unearthing large chunks of concrete.

A row of cars built up behind me. I didn't know which way to turn or whether to go straight through the three-way intersection.

"Crap!" A map of the college, on the passenger seat, didn't help. A rubric of multi-colored squares blurred before me. "Red. Ruth told me to go to the set of *red* buildings."

The car behind me honked. I stepped on the gas and went through the intersection and into the heart of the construction. "Shit."

Hard Hats Required one sign announced. *All Visitors Must Check-In With The Office* another one read.

"Crap, crap, crap." I pulled over to the side of the road,

congested with construction equipment, and men in blaze-orange vests that sparkled in the sun. The reflective safety strips on the vests were blinding.

I held up the map and waited for my eyes to readjust. I took a deep breath and spotted a small cluster of red that appeared to be behind a large green section. The green section, or quad, remained under construction.

"Wonderful." The campus looked infinitely different than when I had interviewed in February. It had been under snow, not construction.

I stepped out of my Suburban and glanced at the curb. It wasn't painted yellow or red. There weren't any parking signs posted.

"What the hell." *It seems to be my mantra since moving back to Casper.*

I reached across the front seat and grabbed my briefcase. The battery in the Suburban's key remote was dead. I hit *lock* on the door handle and bumped it closed with my hip.

I parked on a slight incline. The chunky heels on my platform sandals were new so they seemed to catch every pebble on the graying asphalt. I wanted to make a good first impression so I used my last day of tips at the restaurant to splurge on a lavender paisley-print wrap-around dress and sandals in tawny leather. The combination was contemporary Western chic. Though the buckle closure on the sandals bit into my ankle I walked with the confidence that new clothes brought.

I smiled at the men who stared as I wobbled my way down the sloped road. *Clip clop. Clip Clop. Could I be any louder?* I swallowed a giggle. *Michael's right, I crack myself up.*

The ground rumbled and shook when I approached the health center building. *Just don't fall...that'd suck.* I stopped to view the map and checked my watch again. I had enough time if the administration building truly was just beyond this construction mess.

I hopscotched across the fractured sidewalk that was being splintered by the excavator. A young guy in a hardhat cut the engine.

"Go ahead and pass," he yelled over the drone of the other machines. "I'll wait."

"I'm sorry." I shouted. *Did he hear me? What's the hand signal for thanks?* I made the "A-OK" hand sign when I walked across his construction area looking like a dork.

He jumped out of the cab of his machine and toward the section of sidewalk that was buckled. He was tall, well built and not as young as I first thought. He wasn't old enough to start getting mail from AARP, but he wasn't in his twenties either. For June, the mid-thirty-something year-old was already wearing a good tan.

"I'm sure I'm not supposed to be walking this way." *But now that I have...who are you?*

"You're not the first and I'm sure you won't be the last." He kicked the concrete with his work boot. Dust rose from the gravel nuggets he dislodged.

I waved it away and leaned forward to sneak a peek inside the split in the ground. Chunks of Wyoming's reddish-brown soil were exposed.

"Why are you digging here?"

He tilted his hard hat and wiped his forehead with the back of his hand. His brown eyes contrasted nicely against his blonde hair that was pulled back into a ponytail. "Gas line. We have to cap it before we can continue."

"Makes sense."

"It's a pain in the ass. This University was built back in the day when safety wasn't as big an issue... We've been finding all sorts of lines...that aren't connected to anything, but were buried all the same."

"Oh." I peered deeper into the cavern of exposed earth. "So when you find one of these lines do you have to figure out where it belongs?"

"Shit, yes. It's a mangled mess. Some of these lines aren't labeled so it's like untangling Medusa's hair. We slowly pulled one line out the other day only to find it wasn't hooked up to dick." He shook his head. "I'd like to sit down with the joker who planned this job."

I couldn't stop staring at his ponytail. It wasn't one of those thin, wispy kinds. His hair had a thick luster to it. *Thor. He looks like Thor.*

He pushed a piece of loose gravel into the cavern with his boot.

"Well, I'm glad you're taking your time and doing it right. It'll make me feel safe when I'm in one of these old classrooms. I won't be afraid that with a flip of the switch I'm a goner."

Thor chuckled. "You're a teacher here?"

I blew out a mouthful of air. "If I don't get fired first."

"Where you heading?"

"To this building." I pointed at the map.

"Admin and registration."

I shrugged. "That sounds about right. It's not where I interviewed, but it's where I'm supposed to go." I rubbed my forehead. "I know that makes no sense at all and I probably should have prepared better, but..." I tapped the map with my forefinger. "All I know is that I'm supposed to be at this building," I practically pushed my finger through the map, "to meet and greet students enrolling in my writing class."

He held up his hand in a "Stop" gesture. *Great, I usually don't bore them that quickly.*

"Gimme a minute," he said.

"Okay."

He ran to the other side of the street and hopped into a white motorized cart. He pulled up alongside his excavator.

"Hop in. I'll get you there on time."

"Really?"

"Yeah 'cuz you're not gonna make it wearing those shoes."

I laughingly climbed in beside him. "I'm originally from California. I love Wyoming, but I'm not going to allow it to restrict my wardrobe. I wear boots in the winter, but…"

"Let me guess, they have a high heel."

"Yes, they do. I'm short. I need the height."

He looked over his shoulder for oncoming construction traffic. He pulled into the middle of what remained of the original two-lane road.

"I'm Dani."

"Nice to meet you Dani. I'm Bob."

"Oh my gosh, like Bob the Builder!" My elbow instinctively poked his. "My son loves Bob the Builder."

Bob playfully pushed his elbow back at me. "Do you know how many times I've heard that?"

I clenched my teeth together. "A lot?"

He forced a grin.

"Sorry. I just got excited. It seemed new to me."

He laughed. "I'll live."

Bob pulled up and stopped the cart by the entrance to a glass-fronted building. He cocked his head toward the stairs.

"Use the handrail. I don't want to write up an accident report."

"But I'm a writer I could do it for you." I giggled, but Bob didn't. "Yes sir. I'll use the handrail."

I stepped off the cart and smoothed down my dress.

"Knock 'em dead Dani."

"Thanks Bob the –" I stopped myself. "Thank you." I smiled and he pulled away.

Ruth waited in the lobby of the building. She wore a red polo shirt with khaki colored slacks. Her brownish gray hair was cut short and spikey. "Get lost?"

"I'm sorry. Am I really late?"

"Not at all." She turned toward the elevators. "You've got about a minute to spare."

I groaned. "I'm so sorry."

Ruth laughed. "Listen, this is Wyoming. No one's ever on time."

The door to the elevator opened. I stepped inside behind Ruth. She pushed the button for the fifth floor.

"I hope you don't mind, but I took the liberty of unpacking the books your publisher sent. I put them on display by your table. You may want to change the set-up. Decorating is not my thing."

I smiled. "It's not my strong suit either. My agent calls it *product placement* and showed me a few tricks when she flew out for my first book signing."

"It must be something to be a published author."

I tilted my head toward her. "Thank you, but it was dumb luck really."

"I read *Mercy's Widow*. It wasn't dumb luck. You're a heck of a writer." She studied me with an intense look. "So how'd you learn so much about writing a mystery novel?"

"Research." The answer was automatic. "I couldn't imagine writing without it."

Ruth slowly nodded. "So what kind of research did you do?"

"Oh," I blew out a mouthful of air. "Geez. I interviewed our local sheriff and the deputies in his department to understand police protocol. They introduced me to the county coroner who let me travel with her to Colorado to watch an autopsy."

"You're kidding?" The doors to the elevator opened.

I shook my head, "No. It was amazing."

Ruth extended her hand for me to exit. "So...from all of that you learned how to write a mystery novel?"

I chuckled. "Well, the research helped. It allowed the pieces of the puzzle to fall into place." I stepped into the hallway of the fifth floor. Ruth was on my heels.

"What about the dead body in your book? Is that why you watched an autopsy?"

"Yes and no. I actually learned more from the forensic pathologist who conducted the autopsy. He told me things I didn't know. For instance, that the time it takes for a body to decompose varies based on the conditions surrounding it and stuff like that."

"Huh." Ruth led me toward a conference room. "So...if I ever come across a dead body, you're the person to call?"

I rolled my eyes and laughed. "You'd probably want to call the cops first, but," I raised my finger in the air, "I know enough not to move the body and the importance of evidence. And I'm not so bad at reading a crime scene. There's always a clue, you just have to know what to look for."

Ruth slowly smiled. "Wonderful. Did you keep your notes?"

"From the autopsy?"

"From all of it?" She paused in the middle of the aisle leading to the podium. "Do you still have those contacts?"

I nodded. "Sure. Everyone I interviewed was in the acknowledgements section of my book. Then I went to each of them and gave them a signed copy of my book." A hearty laugh rose from my throat. "I'm not sure how valuable *that* is, but they sure were surprised and grateful. I definitely didn't burn any bridges if that's what you're asking."

Ruth smiled widely. "I can't imagine you'd ever burn any bridges, but it's good to know."

"I can't believe you read my book."

"Well, duh. You're going to be teaching here. And besides," she nudged me, "I couldn't be the only person in town who hadn't read it."

I half laughed. "That's a great thought and very sweet too, but probably not accurate."

"I don't believe that." Ruth cocked her head toward the table with my book display. It was perfectly arranged.

"Thank you." I walked toward it.

"I have to be honest, I didn't know who you were until I went to breakfast with my Saturday group and they about went berserk when I told them I was working with you. You're a big deal."

"I'm not." I stopped walking and Ruth stood beside me. *If I were such a big deal then my husband wouldn't have left me for another woman.* "I got lucky with a book that has been well-received in Wyoming but..." I pushed the strap of my briefcase back onto my shoulder. The weight of the bag kept sliding it forward. "I'm not a big deal." *I'm a recently retired waitress who moonlights as a teacher.*

"Well," Ruth pulled her glasses out of her front shirt pocket and a folded set of papers out of her back pants pocket. "I think you are. And I'm rarely wrong."

I softly smiled. "Okay. I know better than to argue with the woman running the department."

Ruth looked at me over the top of her glasses. "I'm not the director of student affairs. I'm the administrative specialist."

"Sure. And I'm no big deal."

CHAPTER 5

THREE HOURS later when the meet-and-greet wrapped up, I found Bob outside the administrative building.

"Well, aren't you nice?" I stepped into the cart.

"Nah. Don't go tellin' anyone that." Bob veered from the entrance. A bulldozer pulled out in front of him.

My body jerked back and forth with the sudden start and stop movement of the cart. I braced against the front console. "How'd you know when I'd be finished?" *Were you waiting for me? Is this romantic or creepy?*

Bob pressed the cart's accelerator pedal. We lurched back into traffic. "A little bird radioed me."

He waited because he was told to wait. Dang it. I smirked. "A little bird named Ruth? She knows everyone."

"When you've logged the amount of time she has, you will too."

"How long has Ruth worked at the University?"

Bob drummed his fingers on the steering wheel. "Gotta be twenty years now, at least."

"In twenty years, God willing, I'll finally be able to retire just when I'm starting to know my way around this place."

"Yeah and about that time we'll be under construction again."

We both laughed. Bob cranked the steering wheel and whipped the cart around. I grabbed the edge of my seat while the cart skidded up beside his excavator.

"Nice move." I glanced at his parking job and then at his butt in the seat. *Hmmm.*

"Listen." Bob's voice dropped and he glanced over his shoulder. "You said you're a writer."

Yes and single. I nodded. *Did I mention I'm single, too? Can I be single with three kids?* I shook my head. *This is why I'm single…I think too much.*

"Last week, I found something that no one's talking about."

"What'd you find?"

"I'm just thinking that if word got out about this then maybe it wouldn't be brushed under the rug like things tend to be."

"With the University or the construction company?"

"I'm in the maintenance department. The construction company won the building contract because they promised to use the college's classified staff. That way the college doesn't have to employ us year-round."

"Huh." I shook my head. "I'm sorry I got you off track. What'd you find?"

"I don't know anyone who may know what to do with this, but something has to be done with it. I mean…"

"Bob, I'd love to help, but I still don't know how I'd be helping you."

He cocked his head toward a trailer. "It's in there."

"What's in there?"

"I was working the backhoe. I wasn't in this," he pointed to his excavator. "And it's a good thing because I never would've found it. I struck something hard. Usually my blade can cut through anything. But it must've been the angle...or the universe because I finally took a look and I couldn't believe it."

"Bob, you should seriously consider writing mystery novels because you've got the suspense thing down pat. What the *hell* did you hit?"

"Bones."

"Like dinosaur bones? I know the University museum has a ton of them on display. I read something about the area once being a huge stomping ground for wooly mammoths."

Bob gave a curt shake of his head. "The geologist at the museum already looked at them. They aren't the remains of a dinosaur skeleton."

"Then what kind of remains are they?"

"Human."

I stared at the trailer. "Can I go see them?"

"Can you come back later tonight when the construction crew's shut down?"

I must be crazy. "Sure. What time?"

"Make it seven. No, it's still light at seven. Make it eight."

"Should I meet you here?" *Should I wear black clothing? Perhaps a ski mask?*

"Park your car on the road, not on campus. I'll pick you up in the cart."

"This isn't a joke is it, Bob?" *Are you some serial killer and I'm the clueless college coed?*

He leaned toward me and again lowered his voice. "I wouldn't have even told you if Ruth hadn't suggested it."

"She knows?" Relief washed over me. *Ruth would never team up to kill me. She's far too skilled; she'd do it alone.* I smiled.

"She's the one who told me they're covering it up."

"Will she be here tonight?"

"No, but I'm sure she would if you wanted her to."

"I do." I nudged him again with my elbow. "So radio her and get it set up."

"We can't use the radio for this. But she'll be here."

"Then so will I."

CHAPTER 6

MY SISTER, Fiona, read mysteries. She had every Nancy Drew book published and they were now housed on my parents' bookshelf beside my father's collection of academic papers, journals, and textbooks. The yellow spines and Carolyn Keene's name filled an entire row and added the only splash of color in the muted library. The mystery books were cataloged numerically.

I tilted my head to read the titles and then tipped the fourth book forward. *"The Mystery at Lilac Inn."* I smiled at one of the few books I had read about the teenage detective.

"I only read it because it had lilac in the title and I liked the cover."

"Mom?"

I jumped and the book fell off the shelf.

Michael stood in between the sliding doors to my parents' library. His head practically touched the top of the doorframe.

"Are these barn doors?" Michael gripped the side of the heavy redwood paneled door that hung from a wrought-iron piece of hardware mounted to the frame. A pair of rollers allowed each door to slide along the track.

"Yup. They're from the ranch where your Grandpa grew up."

"No way."

I nodded.

"Who knew G-pa was so chill?"

"Right? It surprised me that G-ma let him bring 'em into the house, but then the interior designer had them sanded and refinished and they're beautiful."

Michael tried to palm the side of door. It rolled out of his grip. I tilted my head at him. "Yeah, let's not do that."

He walked into the library and plopped down in one of my father's leather cushioned side chairs.

"How was your day with Uncle Finn?" I sat down in the empty chair beside him. Actually, I fell into the deep cushions. The further I sank the more it felt like a full-body hug. *Who needs a guy when I've got this chair?*

"Oh man, we had a great time. Uncle Finn's so cool."

"He has his moments." I shifted and swung out my leg in an attempt to softly kick my son's chair. *Damn short legs of mine.* I couldn't reach his chair or his leg. I leaned over and swatted his thigh with my hand. "See, I told you things would get better. We just had a rough start that's all."

Michael's eyes welled with tears.

"Hey." I placed my hand gently on his leg.

"I just miss Dad and all my friends." He brushed his cheek against his shoulder. When he resumed eye contact with me his hazel eyes were a camouflage of color swirled together.

"I know." I squeezed his knee and the gesture suddenly reminded me of Gorm. I shook my head. *Focus.* "Michael, it'll get better, I promise. You'll meet other kids your age at football camp and you'll go into high school with a built-in support group."

My son chortled. "Mom, a football team is not a twelve-step

group. I'll be fine. It's just going to take some time that's all." He shifted in his chair and my hand fell aside.

I leaned back in my father's cushioned chair and absorbed the padded softness.

"So who were you talking to?" he asked.

"Uh, no one."

Michael raised an eyebrow.

I rapped my hands against the side of my father's chair. "Oh, okay. I was talking to myself."

"You do that a lot." Michael laughed. The rich sound filled my father's library. "So how was your day at school?"

"Productive. I sold some books, met some students, and it looks like my summer class met its registration requirements so that's a huge relief."

"Don't you get paid either way?"

I chuckled. "No. It doesn't work that way. If my class doesn't hit the required enrollment number they've set, then the University reserves the right to cancel it."

"That's why those in academia, *University professors*, work toward tenure."

My father stood in the doorway. His head actually touched the top of the doorframe.

Great. Here comes the Professor. I took a deep breath. "That's true, Dad. I'm an adjunct so tenure's a bit far from reach right now."

"Daniella, that philosophy is what keeps adjuncts secondary in education." My father gently pulled on the cuff of his fitted gray dress shirt to straighten his already pressed appearance. A glimmer of his silver cuff link made me squint toward him.

There's no way we're related.

"If you only view yourself as supplementary rather than an essential part of the educational process, you will not be seen as anything other than expendable."

"You're probably right, Dad. I…"

"What's the difference?" Michael's voice cut through our conversation. "I don't understand what the big deal is between a *professor* or adjunct."

My father walked into his library. The seams on his black dress slacks broke against his lean legs with each step.

"The difference, Michael," my father's grey-blue eyes narrowed in on my son, "is that one is a profession, a very time-honored profession, and the other is a hobby."

"Wow." I didn't know what else to say. My stomach dropped and so did my heart. *So there it is, the award-winning Professor's view of his daughter. I relocated my children three hundred and fifty miles away from their life for a hobby. Unbelievable.*

I stared past my father to hold back the tears. The paneled wall in the library behind him was adorned with framed degrees and honorary awards for his lifelong achievement as one of Wyoming's premiere professor emeritus' of political science.

"Daniella, it's high time you started considering your future." My father's face remained neutral while he spoke at me. "You are in your forties and time is not on your side."

"Geez Grandpa you make it seem like Mom's over the hill."

The hard lines around my father's eyes softened. He moved toward Michael and positioned himself beside my son. "I'm sorry champ. I worry about your mom."

I watched my son attempt a stare down with my father. "You have a funny way of showing it."

"Michael!" My voice was tight. *I don't need another lecture about rude children.*

"What Mom? If Grandpa really cared he wouldn't put you down. Chase did enough of that for a lifetime…"

My father put his large hand on Michael's shoulder. The

stone in his fraternity ring flashed. "I'm sorry. It was poor of me to talk to your mother that way."

"Don't apologize to me." My son cocked his head toward me. "She's the one you need to talk to."

A firm grin settled across my father's face. "You're right. Daniella?" He stood stoically beside Michael as he addressed me.

I nodded.

"Please accept my apology."

A cold chill shivered through my body. *Do you even know what you're apologizing for?* Still, I did what was expected of me and politely smiled. "It's okay, Dad. I know you only have my best interest in mind."

A pleasing grin crossed his face. "I do." He clapped his hands together proudly. "The sooner we can get your application off to graduate school, the closer you will be to tenure and a future that will make you proud."

You mean a future that'll make you *proud.*

My father walked toward his desk. It was crafted from a rich cut of mahogany with ornate carving on the elongated sides. Claw-footed legs reached out from beneath his desk like a lion guarding its den. I tapped one of the claws with my boots, which I hadn't taken off as per my parent's house rule. *I'm such a renegade.* I shot a glance at Michael. He rolled his eyes.

"I'm sorry, Mom," he mouthed.

I shrugged. *Why? I'm used to it.* I looked at my son. His face carried the one emotion that was foreign to my father: compassion.

"I love you," I mouthed back to my son. Michael grinned and then stood.

"I'm going to go check on James. He wanted to watch a movie. Wanna join us?"

I glanced at my father. He held his chin and intently read something in a vanilla-colored file folder.

"Dad?"

He briefly looked up.

"There was some work I wanted to wrap up at school tonight." *Wait for it.*

My father put down his file.

I smiled. *Bingo. Nothing got the Professor's attention more than talk of academics. Now that I had his rapt attention...* "Would it be okay if the kids stayed with you? I know Mom has her bunko game, but I'd really like to be ahead for my first day of instruction on Friday."

His smile reflected in his eyes. "Daniella, that is very proactive and wise."

Thought you'd approve.

"Yes, it would be a pleasure to watch the children tonight." My father snapped a finger toward Michael. "How about we splurge and order some pizza? I hear Mario's is rather tasty."

"Mario's, huh?" Michael winked at me. "What do you think about Mario's, Mom?"

Gorm. Butterflies suddenly filled my stomach. I grinned at Michael. I hadn't told my parents about Gorm's help in locating Izzy, Mario's pizza or really anything about Gorm. *What would I tell them anyway? That the cowboy next door smelled amazing and looked great in a pair of jeans whether they were clean or dirty?*

I took a deep breath and tried to settle the butterflies before I answered my son. My voice was playful when I did. "Michael, I can honestly say I've never had Mario's pizza before." *Or Gorm for that matter.* "I have, though, heard wonderful reviews, but haven't had a slice myself."

Michael echoed my father's gesture and shot a snap toward

me. "Touché, Mummy, Touché."

My father put his hand to his ear. "What was that Michael? Sometimes this old drafty house makes it hard to hear."

"Nothing Grandpa." Michael spoke loudly. "Mario's sounds great. I'll go tell James."

I watched him leave the library and then redirected my attention toward my father who bent over and picked up the book that had fallen off the shelf.

"Nancy Drew?" He shook his head. "I always thought your sister should be reading something more productive. What is the likelihood of a girl solving a mystery, anyhow?"

He shelved the book and I knowingly smiled. A pile of bones waited for just that likelihood.

CHAPTER 7

So WHAT does one wear when sleuthing? I tapped my chin with my forefinger. The closet in the guest bedroom was larger than my entire bedroom in the townhouse I had just vacated. Mom had hung my clothes on padded hangers and arranged them by color. I was grateful, but annoyed. *Really? Who has this kind of time?*

I slid hangers down the smooth nickel-plated closet rod.

Black. Black. And more black. Nope. Nope. And nope. My life may be in mourning, but I don't have to dress like it. Besides, snooping in black? I shook my head. *Too obvious.*

I moved toward the lighter colored clothing. *It's summer. Be bright and cheery. In other words, fake it.* I skimmed past the softer red and pink tones until I reached the coral colors.

"This is it!"

I gently removed a silk coral tank top off the hanger. I pulled a cream colored cardigan off the closet shelf. The lightweight summer sweater was long and fell open to reveal a hint of coral and my low waisted, boot cut jeans.

I stood sideways in the full-length mirror in the guest

bedroom. My stomach was flat, not quite concaved as I saw in most women's magazines, but it no longer hung over the belt loops of my jeans. My hips were also decisively slimmer since last summer. *Flaunt it if you've got it and I kind of have it...at least when I'm fully clothed. Naked? Another story. Not ready for naked. Why am I even thinking about naked? I'm meeting Bob and Ruth.*

"You look nice." Josie plopped down on the oversized bed we shared.

"It's the divorce diet." I pivoted on the heels of my espresso colored half boots. "It's probably the only upside when your marriage collapses."

"Ahhhh." Josie's compassion stretched out in the long extension of her response. "Mom, that's sad."

I shrugged. "Not really. I can finally fit back into the jeans I wore before I had your little brother."

Josie giggled. "James really turned you into a roly-poly, didn't he?"

I jumped on the bed beside her. "You didn't help either, little one." I buried my head in her stomach and blew a raspberry on her tummy. She squealed in laughter. I continued to tummy torture her.

"Stop it!" she squealed. "No more."

I let her come up for air.

"Geez, all I said is that you were a roly-poly." Her voice was high and tight.

I blew another raspberry. A loud, flatulent sound erupted on her skin.

"Josie! Passing gas is not very ladylike."

She laughed so hard she couldn't speak. She pointed her finger at me. "You did it!"

I sat up and tucked my silk tank top back into my jeans.

"Josie, you'll never get a date being an 'ole gasbag." My head rocked side to side. "Mercy, mercy, mercy."

Josie rolled over and sat up beside me. "You did it."

"I don't know what you're talking about." I straightened my sweater.

"Where you goin'?" Josie asked.

"Can you keep a secret?" I studied her eyes for her reaction. They widened when she nodded.

"I'm going to meet Ruth at the University."

"That's the big secret? Geez. I thought it was something really huge."

"Like what?"

Josie shrugged her narrow, bony shoulders. "I don't know, like maybe you were going to sneak into some building."

I felt my cheeks flush. *Oh my gosh. What does she know? How could she know?* "Why would you think that I'm *sneaking* into some building?" A fake chuckle followed.

"Dunno." Josie leaned back on the stack of pillows that matched the comforter. The bedroom ensemble was part of my Mom's easy living decor. It would've been easy living if arranging the pillows to her liking weren't such an undertaking. I reached behind my daughter and fluffed one of the pillows.

I lightly pushed a finger into her belly. "Tell me what you know and you won't get hurt."

"I don't know anything." She smiled, melting my resolve. It's the effect my kids had on me. *I would move heaven and earth for her. She hasn't ever complained since this whole mess with Chase started.*

"Are you happy we moved?" I asked.

"I miss my friends." She looked down and frowned. Then her head popped up and she quickly added, "but I like that we don't have to drive two hours to go to a mall or to buy groceries."

I laughed. "Staying in the same state to shop is a plus."

"I liked going into Idaho, but it was such a *long, boring* drive."

"And a nightmare in the winter." I shuddered at the thought of black ice; fog and a two-hour car ride just to hit a decent mall and grocery store.

"Heck," I said, "now we live in a thriving metropolis with multiple places to shop."

My daughter and I laughed. Casper was only a metropolis by Wyoming's standards.

"Did you know Grandpa is taking us to get pizza tonight?"

"Yes, and isn't it funny how having pizza two nights in a row doesn't seem to bother you or your brothers."

"Well, this isn't frozen, Mom. Frozen pizza is gross. Mario's is *super yummy* with lots of cheese. I like the plain cheese, but Grandpa said we could have one with cheese *and* mushrooms."

I winced. "Gross. Mushrooms are disgusting."

"Have you even tried them?"

I looked at my daughter. *Who are you?* "You're too rational to be my child. No, I haven't tried them. They're a fungus. Why would anyone try them?"

"Well, you have to give some things a try once in a while."

Josie's brown eyes were full of innocence yet her soul was old.

"You're so beautiful." I brushed hair away from her oval-shaped face. "Inside and out."

We smiled at each other when Michael bellowed from the bottom of the stairs. "Mom!"

I exhaled and jumped off the bed. "Really? Does he think we live in a barn?"

"Grandpa has barn doors in the house. Does that count?" Josie giggled.

I grabbed a pristine pillow off the bed and swatted her. "Enjoy your fungus pizza." I held the pillow ready to wallop her again when Michael hollered. I stopped mid-stream.

"Mom! Gorm's here."

I dropped the pillow and felt the butterflies in my stomach take flight. *What the heck?*

Josie raised an eyebrow and grinned.

"Oh, please. Having him show up is almost as bad as mushrooms popping up on a pizza. Ha!" I started to laugh.

"Mom." Josie's intense brown eyes locked onto me.

"Yes?"

"You have to give some things a try."

CHAPTER 8

"I DON'T even know why I brought you along. I can't *believe* my father asked you to join me." I let out a loud exasperated sigh. "It's not as if I can't find the college by myself. I did it this afternoon. And I'm completely capable of going out at night without an escort."

Gorm leaned his elbow against the armrest on the passenger door and grinned. "Ah, admit it. I'm growing on ya."

"Sure, like a bad rash or something."

"Besides..." Gorm pointed to a side street, "Turn right here. I'm doing a favor for your dad. When he called he said you had some work to wrap up at the college?"

I curtly shook my head. *That was the story I gave the old man to get out of the house.* I made the narrow turn onto Elm Street and glanced at the dashboard. The clock glowed seven forty-five in neon green. "I'm really sorry my dad called and roped you into this. You could have said, 'no.'"

"And miss hanging out with a famous mystery writer? Not a chance."

I chuckled. "Yeah, I'm real famous."

"Besides, you need me."

I briefly glanced at Gorm. "Excuse me?"

"There's the issue of my flashlight. It gets dark on campus. And you never seem to have one." He waved it back and forth. Flashes of yellow glistened like a firefly in the evening sky. His sudden movement released his scent in the car. I deeply inhaled. *What the heck are you wearing?*

Gorm taunted me with the flashlight, but his evasive scent was more teasing.

"I have a flashlight, it's just buried somewhere in a box or maybe..." I quickly looked behind me. "It's in the back."

I stopped at the flashing yellow signal light.

"Um, when it's flashing yellow that means yield. You don't have to stop."

"I knew that." I went through the intersection and slowed down. "Okay, I'm supposed to park somewhere along the street."

Gorm pointed toward a row of trees that bordered the university campus. "That should work."

I inched my car forward until it was beneath a thick cluster of aspen trees, their leaves flitting in the evening wind sounding like coins falling out of a slot machine.

"Quakies."

Gorm looked at me. "They're probably my favorite tree."

"Because they're green?" I didn't even try to hide my smile or my snide tone.

"No. I planted some at my mom's house."

Oh, great, I'm an asshole.

"They don't grow crazy and need trimming," he continued. "They're just simple with white bark and a few leaves, not a lot to rake."

I stared at him. *I am such an idiot.*

He glanced my way and sheepishly said, "And they're pretty

to look at."

It was too dark in the Suburban to see his eyes, but I knew they were shining. Gorm was one of those continually optimistic people. I could just tell.

I unhooked my seatbelt. "Bob said he'd pick me up down here."

"Bob?"

"The builder." I giggled. "I met him today. He's the one who told me about..."

"Yeah, what work do you need to wrap up? You weren't really clear."

"Um..." The yellow-tinted lights from the motorized cart shone through my windshield. "That must be Bob."

I pulled the key out of the ignition and jumped out of the car. I waited for Gorm to exit before I manually hit the lock switch on the inside door handle. *I've got to get a new battery for this remote.*

A larger cart, than the one we shared that afternoon, pulled along the side of the road. Bob stepped out. He seemed taller than I remembered.

"You brought a guest?"

Maybe this isn't a good idea. Did Bob want me alone? Is Ruth a no-show? Maybe I shouldn't have brought a threesome to our twosome?

"Uh," I stammered and then collected my thoughts. "Gorm's my neighbor. Actually he's my parent's neighbor..."

Bob slowly nodded.

Gorm had his hands on his hips. "I wouldn't mind an explanation. What *are* we doing here?"

"You didn't tell him?"

Now Bob and Gorm were staring at me.

"Yeah, well, you suddenly showed up just as I was leaving to go to campus and my dad tells me he asked you to join me. What was I supposed to say? That I was gonna check out some human bones they found at the University?"

"Bones? Human?" Gorm looked at Bob. "What is she talking about?"

Bob tucked his hair behind his ear. It wasn't in a ponytail tonight. It was about chin length with choppy ends. "Look, I'm working construction for the University." He took a deep breath. "I was using the backhoe and hit something. It ended up being a bag of bones."

"They were in a bag? You never mentioned they were in a bag."

The lights from the cart backlit Bob and he was better looking than Thor. His beach-like hair looked naturally kissed by the sun and was messy in all the right parts. When he spoke it moved. "They weren't in a bag per se, but there was an old concrete bag buried beside the bones and we filled it up pretty good."

"Huh." Gorm tapped his flashlight against the palm of his hand. "So you aren't here to work on school stuff?"

"No. That's what I told my dad so he'd watch the kids and I could go out. But apparently he called you to escort me so I wouldn't be alone at night on campus."

"You live with your parents?" Bob had that surfer thing going on. *Is this guy for real? He belongs on a beach not on a backhoe.* Again I watched as he tucked his thick tresses behind his ear. *Momma Mia.*

Gorm lightly tapped my shoulder with the flashlight. "He asked you a question."

"Right." I nodded. "I'm *temporarily* living with my parents. I just moved to town yesterday. I haven't had a chance to do anything, but lose a dog and well, yell at a neighbor."

I sheepishly glanced at Gorm, who was smiling. "I can handle it."

"Oh and now go look at some human remains." *With two very good looking guys.* I threw my hands up in the air for good measure and smiled. "It's been a full forty-eight hours."

I looked at Gorm and then at Bob. *Eenie-Meenie-Minie-Mo...*

A silver SUV pulled up behind my red tank.

"Cheer, cheer the gang's all here." Bob put his hands in his jean pockets.

I watched Ruth climb out of her SUV. She still wore her red polo with olive-colored pants that looked new.

"You look nice," I said as she approached.

"Wore my pocket pants." She pulled a zipper back and forth on her pant leg. "It's got pockets everywhere. They're my casual Friday pants, but I thought I might need to hold something."

I glanced down at my jeans. The pockets were stitched in white thread with Western embroidery running down the side. "I don't think I have any pocket pants, but if I do, I'll wear 'em on Friday."

She slightly blushed and then leaned toward me. "Who's the fella?"

"Ruth, this is Gorm. He's my parents' neighbor and he kind of got roped into coming with me tonight."

Ruth mimicked Bob's initial reaction and slowly nodded. *Maybe it's a college thing.*

"You can trust him. He's not going to tell anyone, are you?" I elbowed Gorm.

"Tell anyone, what?" Gorm scratched his head. "I seriously don't know what the hell we're doing?"

We all smiled and climbed into Bob's cart. Ruth sat beside Bob in the front and Gorm and I claimed the backseat. With each turn, one of us slid into each other.

Butterflies danced a jig in my stomach. *Has it really been that long since I've been touched? A mere bump sends me aflutter?*

The third time we crashed into each other, I couldn't resist a cheesy line. "Is that your flashlight or are you just happy to see me?"

Gorm's deep laugh sounded almost like a growl. *That's sexy as hell.* His entire face lit up. His sapphire eyes twinkled and the apples of his cheeks turned rosy. His whole body embraced the joke. *I made him laugh.* A satisfied grin curved my lips.

Gorm gripped the magnum-sized flashlight. It looked like it was police-issued. "Nah, this is small in comparison."

"Oh, *geez.*" I attempted to swat his leg, but Bob took a tight turn and I ended up grabbing his thigh as an anchor. His leg tightened beneath my hand. A solid mass of muscle filled my palm. *Holy. Hell.* Heat rose between us.

"What are you two doing back there?" Ruth half turned in our direction.

"Nothing." We quickly said in unison.

"Jinx!" I shouted the word I taught Michael and Josie to use when they said the same thing at the same time.

"Really?" Exasperation inched across Gorm's face.

I wagged my index finger at him. "Actually you're not allowed to talk until I release you from the jinx." I sounded like Michael who always beat Josie to the punch and then goaded her.

"I thought the person who was jinxed was supposed to buy the person who called the jinx a pop?" Ruth asked.

I leaned forward and patted her shoulder. "I like your thinking and I think you're right." I bumped Gorm with my hip. "You owe me a soda."

Gorm bumped back. "Really?"

Ruth turned completely around in her seat. "Gorm, it's true.

The penalty for losing a jinx is typically a drink."

Gorm smiled at my colleague. "Okay. Here's the deal. Once we get done investigating or whatever it is we're up to...I'll buy the first round at Murphy's."

Ruth nodded. "It's a deal."

"Murphy's?"

Bob looked at me in the rearview mirror of the double-sized golf-like cart. "It's a tavern downtown."

Again, I hip checked Gorm. "Great. I'll have the largest pint they offer."

Gorm laughed.

"What?"

"Well, Ms. College Professor, there's only one size for a pint and it's sixteen ounces."

"Oh. Well, I'll have whatever's larger than a pint."

Bob chuckled. "You don't go out much, do you?"

"No, I don't. This is the most excitement I've had in a long time." *That I've enjoyed anyway.*

Ruth talked to me over her shoulder. "That's sad."

Bob pulled up behind a gunmetal gray construction trailer and parked in the shadows. A scattering of campus lights and a large flood light bounced off the building under construction.

Bob unhooked his keys that hung from a carabineer latched to one of his belt loops. He held the keys toward the light. He singled one out that glistened and looked like it was cut from nickel. He inserted the shiny key into the lock and the doorknob turned. Bob walked inside. Gorm followed with his flashlight. Ruth and I were the last to enter.

Blueprints and construction plans were held down on a drafting table by a yellow hard hat and a tool belt.

Bob pointed toward a row of cupboards above the sink in the miniature-sized trailer kitchen. Gorm shone his light while Bob opened the cupboard and carefully pulled down a bag.

"I can't believe they just stashed it above the sink? That's so gross. Someone could go looking for Ramen noodles and grab a guy's thighbone. That's disgusting."

Ruth nodded. "That's why we're here."

Bob carried the cement bag that looked like an old gunnysack. He brought it to the kitchen table that had plans rolled up and rubber banded together. Bob untied the twine that held the cement bag together. The bag was in bad shape and the tweed-like material splayed open on the table. Yellow bones spilled out.

I held my breath, but I didn't need to. The bones didn't appear to smell. A musky odor from the decaying gunnysack released. It was rank with mildew.

Bones unraveled beside a skull and jawbone along with a few teeth. The skull looked like it had a missing chunk out of one side.

"What happened to her head?"

Bob looked at me. "Why do you think it's a woman?"

I shrugged. "The skull looks so small."

"I don't think it's all there," Gorm said. "We don't know how large it would have been. Or if it was even prehistoric."

Bob shook his head. "An anthropologist *and* a geologist looked at it. It's definitely human and the anthropologist said the fossils weren't old. More like thirty years old."

"She was thirty?" I asked.

"We don't even know if it's a *she*." Bob's voice rose.

Ruth placed her hand on his arm. "She's asking questions and that's what we wanted. She's a researcher."

"No, I teach a class on researching facts for fiction. I'm not a research scientist. I just know how to weave facts into fiction so it's not boring."

Hearing my credentials or lack thereof made my stomach

and self-confidence take a nosedive. *Why am I here? I've never written about bones. I don't know anything about this.*

Ruth turned toward me. Her face was in shadows, but it was sincere. "I read your book and I now know the research that went into it."

"Oh." My voice dropped. *That's why she was asking me so many questions about 'Mercy's Widow.'*

"Dani, the research and knowledge you gained from that experience are solid. We need you here," Ruth said.

How does she do that? How does she know what I'm feeling? Ruth smiled. *She believes in me.* I felt my eyes well and I hoped no one saw.

I cleared my throat. "Okay, so we don't know if it's a man or woman, but we think the person is thirty?"

Ruth gently touched my arm. "The bones haven't been buried for longer than thirty years. So the consensus was that it was an adult, who was at least twenty."

"Oh. Got it."

"What about the jawbone? There are teeth. Can't they pull dental records?" Gorm asked.

"If they knew what dental records to compare them to." Ruth removed her hand from my arm. "That's the real frustration. No one's doing anything about this. The bones that Bob dug up have literally been shelved."

Gorm scoffed. "Unreal."

"Why would they do that? Don't they have a responsibility to call the police and report human remains?" I seemed to ask more questions than provide answers.

Gorm tilted his head. "Think about it. Why would any prominent university cover up a crime?"

I steadied him in my line of vision. "If it was a crime then they have a responsibility to report it." It was hard for me to imagine that my new employer and my father's beloved University were anything but reputable.

"Dani, please don't tell me your that naïve." Gorm's sarcasm was biting.

"Why is it naïve to think the best of people?" I asked.

Gorm shrugged. "I deal in facts every day. So let's look at the facts. We have a pile of bones that the University had their anthropologist and geologist inspect." He crossed his arms over his chest and buried the flashlight in the side of his hoodie. "The results are that these bones are human. But instead of sending them to the county coroner, they've put them in a kitchen cabinet. Most likely, a rented trailer which could be carted away with the bones when the construction wraps up. Those, Dani, are the facts."

I crossed my arms over my chest and stared back at him. "Those are the *preliminary* facts, but to jump to the conclusion that the university is covering something up is a pretty big leap."

Gorm slowly nodded. "I'm sure the victims at Penn State, whose sexual abuse was covered up by the university for years, hell decades, wouldn't quite agree with your logic. Universities are image orientated. If someone died or *worse* was killed on campus and then their body was buried or *dumped*..." Gorm shook his head. "That's something *any* university would want to keep out of the headlines."

"Which is why neither of you are going to breathe a word of this until we figure out what to do." Bob stood taller than both of us and gazed down at us. "We want your help. We just don't know what's the best way of going about this? If the university is hiding something," Bob flung his hands open, "which it looks like they are. We're not sure how to get them to release the information to the police or the coroner as Gorm suggests."

"Seems to me like you dial nine-one-one and report it."

Gorm's tone turned snarky.

"We thought about that, but..." Ruth's voice trailed off.

Gorm uncrossed his arms and shone the flashlight back on the table. The bones looked brittle. "You don't want to be the whistleblower and lose your job."

"So why did you bring me along?" I held the palms of hands up in a complete surrender. "I haven't even made it through my probationary period. I can't afford to lose my job either." My voice began to sound frantic.

"No one's going to lose their jobs." Gorm remained the voice of reason. "I'm sorry I got everyone riled up. I don't like secrets." His voice was strong and intense. "And *this*," he pointed the flashlight to the table, "is one helluva secret."

We all nodded.

"Do you think there's more?" I gently pulled back the burlap to see the entire remains. The bag had scrunched up and gathered in places. "There's not much there."

Gorm leaned over the table. "Here." He handed me the flashlight. "Will you hold this for me?"

I shined the light toward the table. Gorm gently rolled back the course material and discovered a bump in the fabric. "Something's caught."

Bob's long arms stretched the fabric until Gorm could reach into a small pocket that had formed in the corner of the gunnysack. He pulled out a thin, small bone. Something glistened in the strobe of light.

"What the?" Gorm unlatched the bone from the course material. Something fell back into the cement bag. He reached into the corner.

"It's a ring." He held up a thick gold band with a dark clump protruding from the center.

"Is that onyx or just dirt?" Ruth asked.

He rubbed the ring against his green hoodie. "I think it's some kind of stone," Gorm said and held it back into the light.

The deep, dark velvety blue gemstone shone. "Oh, that's nice," Gorm said. "I'm not sure *what* it is, but it's definitely a gem of some kind."

It can't be. I moved the flashlight closer to the ring. "It's a black sapphire." My voice was barely a whisper. I handed Ruth the flashlight and took the ring from Gorm's hand. I leaned into the light. The black sapphire was dirty, but there was no mistaking the shape and cut of the gemstone. I held the ring and my hand started shaking. *No. No. No.* I looked into the center of the stone and my heart pumped faster and faster. I could feel the beating in my throat. "Oh my God."

"Dani, what is it?" Ruth leaned in closer and tried to gently touch my back, but lost her footing. She fell into me. I dropped the ring and Ruth accidently dropped the flashlight. The heavy stainless steel hit the floor of the trailer. A loud boom rang out.

Bob glanced out the small window in the trailer. "Crap." He flagged his hand toward our circle. "Duck."

We all crouched down beneath the kitchen table.

"Security." He slightly raised his head. "Crap. They're coming this way. Kill the light."

Ruth fumbled to find the switch on the flashlight. Gorm reached across and turned the head of the light into his hoodie. He pressed a button on the side of the flashlight. Instantly the trail darkened. We huddled together under the table.

Gorm leaned toward Bob and whispered, "Did you lock the door?"

Bob shook his head.

Gorm crawled toward the door. A male voice stopped him mid-way.

"Gimme a second. These damn construction kids keep

leaving shit on and unlocked."

Gorm inched closer toward the door of the trailer. He knelt up and quietly turned the lock. He barely removed his hand when the handle turned.

"It's locked." The security guard called out. "Must've been that flood light on the fourth floor. Let's go grab a bite. I'm starved."

Gorm lowered his head and slumped his shoulders forward. I thought he was going to pass out and if he didn't I would. I couldn't stop my rapid heartbeat. Bob snuck a peek out the window.

"We're good," he said.

It was the first breath I drew since Ruth dropped the flashlight.

"We gotta go." Gorm headed toward the door. Ruth stopped him. "We can't leave these bones out."

He exhaled. "You're right. That was just way too close."

We carefully put the bones back into the burlap bag. I looked for the ring, but I didn't see it. I checked the floor, but all I saw was the outline of our shoes. *It must have fallen back into the bag.* Bob tied the gunnysack back together with the twine. He gingerly placed it in the cupboard and looked sternly at me.

"You got your flashlight?" His voice was tense with sarcasm.

It's not my flashlight and he knows it. I picked it up off the floor. Bob opened the door and we all scrambled.

Bob didn't head toward the cart. He motioned for us to follow. We cut through the foliage and down the embankment that led to the street. We actually almost fell through the thick pocket of trees, but when we arrived at the sidewalk we all shared a collective sigh of relief.

"That was too close for comfort." Gorm reached for the door handle of my car. "I can see the headline now, 'Sports Writer

Caught Burglarizing Campus.' Wonderful. I would lose my job."

I clenched my jaw. "I'm sorry. I shouldn't have brought you into this."

Gorm waved away my comment. "I'm a big boy. I could've said 'no' at any time."

Really? You could say no to me?

I unlocked his door. He stepped inside when Ruth approached.

"Let's head over to Murphy's. I think we could all use a drink. Second round's on me."

Gorm raised his eyebrows. "Oh, yeah, I've got the first round with that jinx crap. But," he wagged his finger at Ruth, "You're damn straight, second rounds on you. Butter fingers."

Ruth sheepishly nodded. "You're right. I owe you a tall one."

* * *

Murphy's bar was unusually busy for a Tuesday night, but the crowded space made it easier for us to talk. We filed in and grabbed a corner table next to the bar.

"What the hell happened back there?" Gorm stared at me.

"I'm sorry. The ring surprised me."

"You think?" Bob shook his head and his hair moved like a rolling wave across his face. "It surprised all of us."

"It surprised the flashlight right out of my hands," Ruth joked.

"That wasn't funny." Gorm shot her a serious look.

"Oh, relax," she said. "We all got out of there just fine." Ruth elbowed me. "So what was up with the ring?"

I took a drink and wiped my mouth with a bar napkin. The image of my lips stained the napkin red. *Chase used to love it when I did that.* I looked across at Gorm. He focused on me, not the napkin. *Is that a good or bad thing?*

"Uh...I wasn't sure at first...but then I was." I stammered.

"Cryptic. Perfect." Gorm brushed his thumb against his frosted beer mug. It was almost empty. "Par for the course."

"I'm not trying to be cryptic." I scratched my head. "I had to be sure and now I am."

"Sure of what?" Bob's hair now moved like a tidal wave along with his escalating mood.

Oh geez. Just spit it out. Where do I start? I took a deep breath before continuing. "If you looked closely, in the center of the stone, there's a coat of arms."

"What?" Gorm motioned his beer mug toward the waitress.

I slowly exhaled. "Inside the coat of arms were the Greek letters X, Y, Z."

"Ohh-kay." Gorm leaned over in his chair and shook his glass again at the waitress. "And what does that mean?"

"In Greek, it means Xi Upsilon Zeta, but the 'Y' can be used as either a 'Y' or a 'U' in the Greek alphabet."

"Again? What does that mean? And why does it matter?" Gorm finished off his pint and handed it to the waitress in exchange for another.

I handed her my empty mug and received another microbrew.

"Is that some fraternity or something?" Bob's tone softened and his hair fell forward and hung perfectly around his face.

"XYZ? I've never even heard of it." Gorm hoisted his red ale to his mouth.

I tried to match Gorm beer for beer so I took a big swig. The cool hops hit my empty stomach. The beer settled and warmed me from the inside out. I held my mug out in front of me. *That's some good shit.* There wasn't any nasty barley taste at the back of my throat.

Gorm momentarily laughed. "Not bad, is it?"

I shrugged and then smiled. "It's freakin' delicious."

"Hello. Beer *connoisseurs* can we get back to the little XYZ thing?" Bob's voice regained its tension.

"Right." I placed my mug on the table. "The little XYZ thing is based off the XYZ Affair."

Gorm, Ruth and Bob stared blankly at me.

"You know, when the French demanded a bribe from the United States before they'd begin negotiations with us."

"Great a history lesson, but what does this have to do with the ring?" Gorm's blue eyes took on an icy stare.

"It's an academic fraternity. Actually, XYZ is the name a group of political science majors created when they formed their own fraternity."

Gorm rolled his eyes. "How can you be so sure?"

"Because my father has the same ring."

CHAPTER 9

Bob AND Gorm leaned against the outside of the bar's brick façade debating who was looking better for the fall, top-ranked University of Oregon or second-seated Stanford. Gorm tucked his hands in his green Oregon hoodie, which punched the duck in the center of the sweatshirt forward. Bob, a California native, listened intently to Gorm's argument, but leaned heavily toward The Cardinals.

While they bantered, Ruth nodded toward my car. "I'll walk with you."

I squinted looking for where it was parked.

"It's across the street next to the bank." Gorm called out from the side of the building.

"Got it." I waited for a car to pass before Ruth and I jaywalked.

"Hey look at that. We're breaking another law." I watched the two-way street for any traffic.

Ruth chuckled. "I told you I was a bad influence."

I laughed. "I must have missed that lecture."

Ruth stepped onto the sidewalk. "Lecture? Ouch. I hope I don't lecture."

I reached out to touch her and grabbed air. *Maybe matching Gorm in beers wasn't such a good idea.* I resumed, what I hoped looked like walking, beside Ruth. "Oh, you don't lecture. It was a poor choice of words."

I glanced over my shoulder at the guys. Gorm's hands were out of his pocket and in the air. "Uh-oh. Bob must have blasphemed Oregon."

"So who do you like better? Shaggy or Chuck?"

I whipped my head around toward Ruth. The sudden spin caused me to see two of her. I shook it off. *Focus. Focus. Focus. Okay, the 'Shaggy' reference has to be about Bob.*

"Chuck?" I asked.

"With that pumpkin-shaped head don't you think he looks a little like Charlie Brown?"

"Oh you're awful but ..." I started to giggle. "Come to think of it...yeah, he does look a bit like the round-headed kid."

I glanced again across the street. Gorm was animated when he spoke. His solid build and flashes of temper reminded me of a passionate Italian. His last name though didn't mesh with that lineage. *Gorham? Is that Dutch? Hungary? Or is it Hungarian? What the hell does it matter when it's always Gorm that captures my eye?*

I massaged the back of my neck. "Oh, I'm not interested in either of them."

Ruth blew out a mouthful of air. A puff followed. "Sure. And I'm Annie Oakley."

"Nice to meet you Annie, I'm Dani. Hey—" I bumped against Ruth's hip. "That rhymes. Annie and Dani."

Ruth wore a solemn expression. "I'm not amused." Though she couldn't hide her pending smile.

"You *so* don't have a poker face. You know that, right?" My words began to slur. *How much did I drink?*

"That's why I play dice."

"Too much math for me." I slapped my leg and snorted. "I crack myself up."

"Either that or it's the four pints you drank. Are you okay to drive?"

"I'm fine." Again I tried to touch her shoulder and instead it looked like I was swatting a fly. I cleared my throat. "Honestly, I sweated so badly in that trailer I think the beer replaced my lost fluids."

Ruth nodded.

"I'm not kidding. I'm okay. The trailer part, though, was pretty hairy."

Again Ruth nodded.

"Suddenly you're so quiet?"

Ruth tilted her head toward the northern sky. I looked up. Stars scattered across the midnight horizon stretched as far as the eye could see. Casper Mountain, in the distance, was a silhouette against the darkened sky.

"There's no place like Wyoming," I said.

"You got that right kid."

Ruth and I walked the last hundred yards to my car in silence. I put my key into the door. "I think I'll wait a few minutes and then drive around and pick up Gorm."

"That's a good idea." Ruth crossed her arms over her chest. "Listen, that business about the XYZ fraternity, do you know if your father has a roster or list of alumni?"

"Huh." I went through his library in my mind. "I know he has his college yearbook...but...I don't remember ever seeing anything about the fraternity. He's pretty hush-hush about the whole thing."

Ruth cocked her head. "Really?"

"All I know is that the fraternity wasn't sanctioned by the

school and that it was underground."

"That doesn't sound like something a professor emeritus would be involved in."

I brought my shoulders up to my ears. The warmth felt good. "Your right, it doesn't sound like something my father would do *today*, but from what my mom tells me he was quite the renegade back in the day."

Ruth rubbed her shoe on the pavement like she was extinguishing a cigarette.

"Was it something I said? I love my dad, we just have a difficult..."

Ruth exhaled. "Dog-gone."

I chuckled. "Watch your language there, Missy."

She slightly smiled. "Listen, you'll find out soon enough, but I knew your dad 'back in the day'."

"Huh. I didn't know." I felt myself begin to wobble. I opened the door to my car and plunked down in the driver's seat. "How did you know my dad?"

"I was in my first year of grad school when the University hired him to teach. He went on to begin his doctoral studies, but before he did he was a helluva good professor."

"So I've been told – repeatedly." I leaned my head against the steering wheel. I spoke into the black molded plastic. "And I'm sure I'll hear more about it when I begin teaching." I raised my head and pointed my finger at Ruth. "You know it's no picnic being Joe Quinn's kid." I chuckled. "That almost sounded like a lot of alliteration, and that would be bad." I shook my finger and scolded my colleague. "Alliteration is very, very bad."

"Ohh-kay. I think someone's had too much to drink." Gorm walked up behind Ruth and patted her back. "I'll make sure she gets home safely."

He reached into the car for the keys. I leaned forward and

bumped into him. His smell was as inviting as the micro-ale. "You're delicious." My voice echoed my mood—dreamy and soft. I looked into his eyes and he started to chuckle.

I snapped back against the car seat and felt heat rise to my face. "I meant, the beer, the beer was delicious."

Ruth howled. "So Chuck it is."

CHAPTER 10

"So..." I leaned over the passenger seat and inched up beside Gorm.

A long *yes* followed along with his captivatingly seductive smile.

I walked my fingers up the sleeve of his hoodie and stopped at his chin. It was grizzly and needed a shave. I turned his chin toward me. "Wanna play?" My eyebrows arched along with the curve of my lips.

He opened his mouth and tried to bite my finger.

"Hey!" I withdrew my hand in surprise. *Well, well, well.*

"I thought you wanted to play?" He coyly smiled and I felt my stomach stir with emotion.

"Not like that!" I swatted his shoulder. *Well, kinda like that.* I snickered to myself.

Gorm turned the key and started the Suburban.

I groaned. "Ohhh, I don't want to go home yet." *I wanna have some fun. Some good 'ol fashion dirty fun.*

"Who said anything about going home?"

The butterflies in my stomach fluttered. I smiled so wide it hurt my cheeks. *Maybe this night will be fun after all.* I turned on the radio. A hip-hop song bounced its beat out of the speakers. I started to sway in the seat.

"Please don't tell me you like this shit?" Gorm leaned toward me waiting for a response.

"This is great. Don't you love the beat?" I snapped my fingers. "It's about a girl that meets a guy and wants him to call her."

"Wow. That's original. That's just...wow, I don't know what to say to those lyrics."

I bobbed my head and rose to my knees in my seat. I turned my body toward Gorm. Only the center console separated us. *Why didn't we take your Jeep? That has a huge bench seat and a whole lotta room.* I rolled my shoulders toward him. He grinned. I gyrated my hips to the beat of the music and threw my head back.

"Do you even know how cool this song is?" I inched toward him a little more, but in my attempt at drunken seduction, I leaned too far forward and fell. Gorm reached out both arms and caught me before my stomach slammed against the console. I landed softly against him. For a moment, I closed my eyes and breathed him in. *How can this already feel so right?*

"Uh-oh." I giggled. "I think that last beer got me." I tried to push myself up off Gorm. His chest felt as solid as his legs. *This guy's seriously built. I would love to climb him.* I placed my hands firmly against him, but my knees locked behind the console. I couldn't get any leverage to separate us. I was laying on Gorm and the console, with my knees still bent on the passenger seat that seemed to have buckled behind me. *Awesome.*

"It's a real twister, isn't it?" I chuckled and again tried to extricate myself from Gorm, but whatever stomach muscles I had were suddenly dormant. I crashed back into him. "I'm snuck. I mean stuck." I snorted when I laughed.

"That's hot."

I buried my head in his chest and squealed. "You weren't supposed to hear that." *Like ever.*

He whispered in my ear. "No, that's *hot.*"

I lifted my face toward him.

"Those eyes." He softly held the sides of my face, pulled me up toward him and kissed me. His lips were soft. I dislodged one of my knees from the console and climbed over and onto him.

I straddled him in the driver's seat. His hands gripped my hips and pulled me toward him.

"You're so damn sexy." He locked his glassy blue eyes on me.

This time I held his face and pressed my mouth against him. Our tongues collided and explored each other. When we pulled away, I was inches from his face. I stared at his lower lip. It was full and pouty. *Yum. Yum. Yum.* I nibbled on it while his hands explored me.

I made my way to his neck and inhaled his spiciness. I closed my eyes and this time when I breathed him into me I let him fill every pore. *If this is all I get, I want it all.*

He grabbed my ass. "I just wanna spank you." His voice was deep and wrought with desire.

I giggled. "So..." I looked up at him. "You're an ass man?"

He shook his head and his cheeks flushed. "No, not at all."

I pushed myself down on him and grinded. "Sure. You just wanna *spank me.*"

He pulled away from me and rested his hands back on my hips. "No, I didn't mean that. It just... I'm not some freak."

I leaned toward him and whispered in his ear. "Bummer."

He raised his pelvis and slammed my hips down onto him. Our bodies struck in all the right places. The heat from his groin rammed against me. *Hello, Cowboy.*

"Is that for me?" I coyly looked at him.

"Does anyone ever say *no* to you?"

I slowly swayed my head to the beat of the next song on the radio.

"You're trouble."

I moved my head up and down and raised an eyebrow. "You have no idea."

I reached between my legs and cupped the crotch of his jeans. He tilted his head back against the seat. A low sexy murmur rose from his throat.

I glanced down. His belt buckle was like any other cowboy buckle. It had taken me years to figure out that a cowboy buckle consisted of three pieces: the buckle, the tip of the belt and the piece that held the end of the belt. Gorm's belt buckle was silver with lots of Western engraving, but it nonetheless opened with a synch of the wrist. I pulled it back, unsnapped the tip of the buckle and viola it sprang open.

"Thing of beauty," I said with a mischievous grin.

I leaned toward Gorm. He moved to kiss me. I pulled away and shook my head. He tilted his head in question.

I pressed against him and slid my hand down the side of the driver's seat. I hit the button that moved the seat back.

"Oh, you're good," he said as we glided back until the seat couldn't go any further.

"This ain't my first rodeo, Cowboy."

He smiled. "Smart girl." Gorm grabbed my ass and pulled me toward him. "Git on over here."

I sat up on him and arched my back. My sweater slid down my arms and my silk tank top stretched tightly against my breasts. My hair danced on my naked shoulders. Gorm reached up and buried his hands in the waves of curls.

I slid between his legs and knelt before him. My back was pressed against the steering wheel. I crawled toward him. I lifted his hoodie from the top of his pants with my teeth and found a toned, muscular chest with dark hair. I kissed his broad chest and inhaled him. He was intoxicating to the senses.

I trailed my tongue down his body to the fine line of hair that began at his navel and was interrupted by his worn jeans that were partially open. I tugged on the metal tab on his zipper until it slid down with an unmistakable zip when it released. I reached down between us and released him in my hands.

Gorm raised his hips and I lowered his jeans to reveal a thick patch of hair that carried the same spiced aroma as his chest. I burrowed my nose in his groin.

Jackpot. I was pleasantly surprised by his grandeur. I looked up at him and my face must have revealed my satisfaction. He returned my smile.

"You expected anything less?"

I shook my head as I gently cupped him in my hand and kissed him and stroked him with my tongue.

He dug his hands in my hair and groaned. "God, Dani..."

If there was one sexual talent I had it was having perfected a blowjob.

"No one's ever been able to..." his voice trailed off.

I looked up at him and reached my finger to his lips. "Shhh."

I returned to stroking and sucking him. My mouth and hand worked in perfect synchronicity.

The beat of the music combined with Gorm's guttural moans was electrifying. I was on fire.

Gorm's thighs tightened and his hands gripped my shoulders. "Oh, my God, I'm com..." He suddenly jerked forward in the seat. My mouth and hand never wavered. I sucked him until he exploded in my mouth.

"Oh, my God!" His legs quivered. "Oh, my God."

His whole body shook.

I swallowed and looked up at him.

"You're amazing." His entire body relaxed beneath me.

I smiled with my eyes. *Yeah, I still got it. That's right Cowboy I am amazing.*

"I mean it. No one's ever been able to do that. It was like an urban legend I only heard was possible." He leaned his head back against the seat. "Oh my God that was...surreal."

I crawled up between his legs and leaned toward him. The sweet, tangy scent of sex lingered between us.

"Get over here." He pulled me onto him. I pressed against his chest. He kissed me with such intensity it compounded the heat between my legs.

He pulled away and looked at me. "I'm usually not that selfish."

A wide smile filled my face.

"You're amazing." Admiration clearly shone in his eyes.

I shook my head. "No, you had it right the first time."

A puzzled look flashed across his face.

"I'm trouble." *Big trouble, buddy. Like not even sex will make it worth it.*

"Nothing I can't handle." He kissed me again.

I straightened my tank top and pulled up my sweater. "We'll see." I winked at him and felt the butterflies start to retreat. *I want to believe you but...I've made that mistake before.*

I was climbing back over the console when he grabbed my arm and spun be back toward him.

"Dani, you'll see that not only can I handle you..." He pulled me into him.

I caught my breath.

"But you'll like it."

CHAPTER 11

GORM PARKED my Suburban in my parents' driveway. I barely waved goodbye when he began his trek toward his house.

"Don't worry 'bout me," he said in a low, yet audible voice.

I turned around. His gentle face shone in the moonlight. *I think I'm falling for him.* I stared at him afraid to look away and lose this feeling of perfectness.

"I don't mind doing the walk of shame." A goofy look crossed his face. "It's been a while, but I can live with it."

I couldn't help but laugh.

"Oh, quit it." I waved my hand toward him. "The walk of shame is if you came home tomorrow in the same clothes you wore today."

Gorm stepped back toward my parents' house that activated the motion-sensor light on their garage. The stream of light touched the top of his head and made it look like he was an apparition. I blinked, but he still looked like a spirit. *I will never drink this much again. Like ever.*

"Dani," he said with a wry grin, "it *is* tomorrow and I'm still in the clothes I wore yesterday. So are you."

"Huh." I looked down at my clothes and began to wobble.

"Easy there, Tex." He put his hands out ready to catch me again even though I wasn't within arms' reach.

"Wyoming." I wagged a finger at him. "I'm not from stinkin' Texas." I slapped my thigh and snorted when I laughed.

"God, you're sexy."

I giggled when I shooed him away. "Shh!" A little spit flew out of my mouth when I laughed a second time. *Crap. Please dear God don't let him see that I'm drooling.* I casually wiped my mouth against my shoulder and smiled. "My parents are sleeping." *I did not just say that. How old am I?*

Gorm made the same "A-OK" symbol with his hand like I had with Bob. For some reason him mimicking my gesture made me howl out and laugh.

He hurried toward me and put his hand over my mouth. "You're gonna get us both in trouble."

I tried to bite his hand. He pulled it away and pressed his mouth against mine. He tasted sweet. No matter when I kissed him, and it hadn't been many times, he always tasted sweet.

"Tuck me in bed," I said when our mouths parted.

"You have no idea how much I want to do that."

"Sure, sure, sure." I pushed him away. "Now that you've had me..." *You won't want me.*

Gorm pulled me back toward him. "Dani, I'll say it until you hear it. I'm not going anywhere."

I stared into his blue eyes. "I know." I paused and for a moment I felt very sober. "That's what scares me."

He held me against his chest and spoke into my hair. "I don't know about those other guys and I really don't want to know. I'm here now. And I'm not leaving."

I looked up at him. "Except to go home because if my dad sees us together he'll freak."

Gorm grinned. "Don't be so sure. Your dad likes me."

"He likes me too, but that doesn't mean he always likes the choices I make."

"Trust me." he said and then kissed me. "Git on home, now." He patted me on the butt.

Gorm waited until I was inside my parents' house and had turned off the porch light. I snuck into my father's library. I sank in one of his side chairs and watched Gorm out of the large front window until he was a blurry shadow in the distance.

A slight breeze filtered into the library from the top window —the only other relic my father had acquired from his childhood. I've often thought that my parents' entire house was built around this one window. The retractable window ran the length of my father's study. The window was from the old schoolhouse that my father attended and his mother had taught at. Its placement in the front room was clearly a focal point for passerby's and oddly transformed this one section of the house to resemble my grandmother's one-window classroom.

I squinted at the upper window. It added light, even moonlight, to the room, but somehow kept the rain out. It had to be the slanted opening. Rain cascaded down the exterior single pane of glass, but nary a drop rolled inside.

There was a bronze handle in the center of the window. A simple twist of the handle followed by a slight push and viola the window popped out to open.

I never had any luck getting the window open. I was hoping it'd be easier to close. The June air had a bite that chilled. *Funny, I wasn't ever cold when I was with Gorm.*

The thought of him made my footsteps light as I walked toward the adjacent wall. I dragged over the other side chair and kicked off my boots. I stood on the edge of the chair, leaned forward and rose on my tiptoes until I could reach the window and grab hold of the bronze handle.

The chair began to wobble and I started to lose my grip.
"Damn it."

I didn't know whether to let go of the handle and fall forward
and possibly crash into the solid sheet of glass beneath the
schoolhouse window. Or, let my feet slide the rest of the way off
the chair and hope the handle could hold my weight.

Decisions. Decisions. I started to giggle and I couldn't stop.
I was deliriously tired and still more than a bit tipsy. I swayed
slightly while I held the handle and teetered on the chair.

My weight made the decision for me when the window
suddenly slammed shut. I was bucked off the handle and chair
simultaneously. Somehow I made a perfect dismount from both,
landing in between the front window and the chair without
wrecking either one.

I proudly raised my arms in the air like a gymnast after a
solid routine on the balance beam.

"Ten. Russia gives her a ten. Or is it The Soviet Union?" I
fanned the air. "Hell, the Eastern Block gives her a ten."

I laughed so hard I couldn't breathe. I plopped down on the
floor. There were three built in shelves beneath the window seat
in my father's library. I tilted my head against it and rolled my
head from side to side. My neck cracked as tension released.

What a day. Bones. Beers. Blowjob. I held up a finger. *But
only one blowjob.* I chuckled and then looked up at the ceiling.
What the hell was I thinking?

I yawned and stretched my arms out. *I need to get to bed.*

I leaned on the window seat to push myself up, but my hand
slipped and I hit one of the drawers beneath it, which rolled
open. Red albums with gold edged embossing were perfectly
stacked in neat rows.

They looked like our family photo albums. *I thought they
were blue, not red.* I reached in and pulled one out. The musty

smell of mildew made me turn my head. *Damn. It's just like the bag of bones. What the hell?*

The arid, sharp bite of mold hung in the air. I shuddered. "That's awful." I rolled out the entire shelf and palmed the drawer for water, but it was dry.

"What the heck?" I cracked the album. Even in the moonlight, the water stains that riddled the pages were visible. "Oh, no."

I walked to my father's desk and turned on his reading lamp. It cast enough light to look at the album without alerting anyone that I was still awake.

A picture of my mom and dad curled along the edges. I tried to smooth it out, but the picture coiled back to its ruined state. *What a shame.*

I flipped through the pages.

"That's weird." Instead of the pictures getting older as the pages progressed, they decreased in age and my mom disappeared from view.

The back section was filled with pictures of my father in college. I turned the album horizontally to look at an eight-by-ten sized black and white photograph.

Four beautiful women in black cocktail-style dresses sat at a round banquet-style table. Four men stood behind them. A fifth man, my father, stood off to the side beside a man who had his hand on the shoulder of the most striking woman in the picture. She radiated. Her beauty was breathtaking.

I carefully removed the photo from the four black photo corners that held it against the black parchment page in the album.

The three other women smiled and looked happy. Yet despite the fourth women's exquisite beauty, there was a sadness to her that was palatable on the page. *What's her story?*

I stared at her and then at the man behind her. He was tall, broad-shouldered and well built. My father looked handsome, but this man was dashing. I leaned toward the picture. *He looks so familiar.*

I shook my head and rubbed my eyes.

"It can't be."

I squinted at the man's hand on the woman's shoulder. A fraternity ring like my father's was on his right ring finger. I glanced at my dad. His left hand was down at his side and not visible. But his right hand was barely tucked into the pocket of his white dinner jacket. The dark stone from his fraternity ring caught the camera's light.

I quickly scanned the other three men. Two of them wore the same ring. I scratched my head. "Oh my God. Is this the fraternity? Are these are the men of XYZ?"

"Dani?"

I heard my father's voice from the stairway.

I slid the photo under his desk blotter and quickly turned off the reading light. *He'll wonder what I'm doing in the dark.* I turned it back on and put the album back in the window drawer. I quietly rolled it closed and jumped into the side chair just as my father walked into his library.

"Daniella, is that you?"

I turned toward him. "I'm sorry, Dad. I couldn't sleep. I thought I'd come down here and grab a book."

Shit. Shit. Shit. I'm still in yesterday's clothes. "And I can't find where Mom put my pajamas."

I nervously laughed.

My father slowly nodded and then smiled. "Your mother is nothing if not efficient. I am sure your laundry is pressed and folded in a drawer somewhere."

"Oh, you're probably right."

My father walked toward me. My heart began to race. "Have

you tried Dickens?" He brushed past me and toward his library of books. "I always thought he could put anyone to sleep."

My relief came out as a loud laugh. "Huh." I stood up and walked over to my father. I slightly elbowed him. "Who knew my dad had a sense of humor?"

He put his hand on my shoulder like he had with the man beside him decades ago in the photograph. I stopped breathing. *He saw the picture. Crap.*

"There are many things you don't know about me." He squeezed my shoulder. "They aren't all bad either, Daniella."

I looked up at my larger than life father. *Why can't you always be like this?* I barely leaned my head against him. "Thank you for letting my children and me stay here."

He turned me toward him and planted a hand on each of my shoulders. "You are my daughter. You are my blood. I may not always like or even approve of your decisions, but they are yours to make. You never turn away from your family."

I closed my eyes to stop from crying. I felt him gently kiss the top of my head. I opened my eyes and he handed me Dickens. "Trust me. This will put you to sleep in a second."

It was the second time that night when a man told me to trust him. This time I had no choice. I took the book and turned off the reading light before my father could see the edge of the photo sticking out from beneath his desk blotter. I grabbed my boots and followed him upstairs. He returned to his bedroom as quietly as he had exited.

I shut the door to the guest room and tossed Dickens on my daughter's pile of clothes. I shimmed out of my jeans, pulled off my sweater and tank and unhooked my bra and replaced them with oversized sweats and a softly worn sweatshirt. I crawled into bed and curled up next to Josie.

Wake up before Dad. Hide the picture before he sees it...

CHAPTER 12

BLANKETS PULLED up to my chin; my head cradled by an oversized feather pillow. With the exception of Josie's foot pressed against my back, I was in a state of bliss. I slowly woke when I heard James, less than subtly, tiptoe along the hardwood floor in the guest bedroom. With my eyes sealed shut, I smiled at the sound of my five-year-old approaching. *Here he comes.*

He stepped on the bed railing and pressed against the mattress. He leaned over and kissed my cheek.

I opened my eyes. His grey-blue eyes widened and he softly smiled. "You're awake."

I nodded and put my finger to my lips. "We've got to be quiet, Josie's still sleeping."

James shook me. "But we're going swimming!"

I rubbed the sleep out of my eyes and wiggled myself into a sitting position without forfeiting the warm blankets around me.

"Swimming?" I whispered.

James nodded. "Yeah! Grandpa's talking to that guy downstairs."

"What guy?"

"You know Goldberg."

I laughed. "You mean Gorham." My body flooded with the sensation of his body close to mine. Heat rose from beneath the sheets.

"Yeah, he's having coffee with Grandpa."

"Right now?" Panic seized my throat. "He's *here* right now?"

I started combing my hair with my fingers like my teenager did. *Crap. Why is he here?* The heavy burden of regret sank to the bottom of my stomach. I closed my eyes. *Last night. Oh my God. I went too far.* Memories came flooding back along with shame. *Why did I do that? What is he going to think of me?* My eyes burned. *Do not cry. James cannot see that. Get it together. It was only one night.* I opened my eyes and looked at my son.

"Well, then I guess we'd better go see what this is all about." I poked him lightly in the tummy. "Swimming, huh?"

James started to hop up and down. "Swimming!"

I don't even know where my suit is. Is it on the moving truck? Did I pack it? Crap. I'm not swimsuit ready. Granted, I look better than I have in a while, but I'm not ready for this. That's why I kept my clothes on last night.

Gorm and my father sat at the breakfast bar with a pot of coffee between them.

"Good morning, Daniella. I wanted you to meet our neighbor, Chris."

Gorm stood up when I walked toward them.

"Dad, I met Gorm when we arrived. And you sent him with me to campus last night, don't you remember?"

My father's face was unnervingly blank.

"Remember, he came to my rescue with the house key and then again..."

Gorm cut in. "You didn't need rescuing."

I tilted my head at him. *He remembered my rant. How sweet.* "Well, he's been super helpful, huh, James?" I glanced down at my preschooler who was hanging on our every word.

"Yup. Goldbug was great."

"Gorham." I quickly corrected. "It's not Goldberg or Goldbug. It's Gorham. Or Gorm."

Gorm chuckled. "James, I answer to a lot of different names."

I tensely smiled. "I'm sorry. He's just…"

"He's six?" Gorm asked.

"Five." My father scooped him up and put him on his lap. He jostled him up and down. "That I haven't forgotten. My grandson is fantastically five. And the last grandchild if I'm not mistaken?" My father looked at me.

"Yes, dad. James is your last grandchild."

He let out a noticeable sigh of relief.

I rolled my eyes and reached for a cup from the coffee tree that was positioned off to the side on the breakfast bar. Gorm grabbed the coffee pot. "May I?"

I gave him a saucy wink. "You may." *You may indeed.*

He poured coffee, but stopped mid-way from the top of the mug. "I left room for cream."

I blushed. "Yeah, my sister, Fiona, says I like hot cream." *Oh crap.* I quickly made eye contact with him. *That came out wrong.* I cleared my throat. "Because I use so much milk in my coffee." I dropped eye contact with Gorm and stared into my coffee.

Thankfully my father was busy playing patty-cake with James.

Gorm reached past me for the mini-carton of milk and brushed my arm. Electricity buzzed between us. "Hot cream, huh?" he whispered.

I elbowed him and he almost dropped it. "Knock it off," I

mouthed.

His eyes twinkled.

I shook my head. "You're impossible."

"What's that?" My father redirected his attention toward me.

"It's impossible, I was saying, to go swimming today. James said something about it and I don't even know where our suits are. I think they're in a box on the moving truck."

My mom walked into the kitchen. The breakfast bar separated the two spaces. She flung a dishtowel over her shoulder and began unloading the dishwasher.

"Dani, Finnegan bought the kids swim suits yesterday and your high school swimsuit is still upstairs in your dresser."

"Mom! I can't wear that. It's like twenty years..." I stopped mid-sentence. I didn't need Gorm to know exactly how old I was. *Keep something sacred.*

"Dani, you have a beautiful figure and you're such a talented swimmer." My mom leaned over the kitchen sink toward the breakfast bar with an oval-shaped baking dish in her hand. She dried it while she spoke. "Christopher, did you know our Dani went to college on a swimming scholarship?"

Gorm bobbed his head. "Wow. I did not know that."

"It's probably the only thing she didn't tell you," I said under my breath.

"No, there's quite a bit I didn't know about you," Gorm said quietly as he reached for his cup of coffee. "Like how hot you are."

I wanted to elbow him again, but both my parents stared at me.

"Swimming, huh?" I raised my voice to drown out Gorm's. "Where are we going?"

"Paradise Valley has a lovely swimming pool. A few water slides and high dives. The kids will love it. And," my father patted me on the back, "a good workout will help you sleep better tonight."

Gorm almost spit out his coffee.

My father leaned past James, who was still on his lap, and spoke to my mother. "I found Daniella in the library and it was well past three in the morning. Poor thing couldn't sleep. She was still in the same clothes she wore the day before."

Gorm started to choke and hit his chest with his fist. "Went down the wrong pipe."

"Yeah, that can happen," I said and shot him a sly wink. "You've really got to be careful not to put too much in your mouth." *Two can play at this game.*

Gorm's cheeks reddened and a crooked smile filled his face. "I'll remember that."

"Christopher, you'll join us, won't you?" My mom put the baking dish in the cupboard and looked up for his reply.

"Of course he will. It'll be our treat. It's our way of thanking him for helping Daniella last night on campus." Pride returned to my father's face.

Gorm volleyed his attention between my parents and landed his gaze on me. "Is that alright with you?"

I tried not to smile, but I couldn't help myself. "Sure." *Getting to stare at your bare chest and legs all day? What's not right about that?*

"Great." Gorm clapped his hands together. "It'll be fun to chase everyone around in the water."

Oh, you have no idea.

"Well, be warned..." I turned and held my arms out for James. He leapt into them. I looked over my shoulder at Gorm as I walked away. "No one's ever been able to catch me."

CHAPTER 13

I GRIPPED the sides of the starter's block and waited for the imaginary sound of the gun. *Bam.* I lunged forward, arms straight out in front of me, head tucked, body tight. The cold water bit the top of my head and cascaded over my body in a ripple that sent a jolt down my spine.

I held my arms out in front of me and gripped my hands together while my body swayed rhythmically. Two strong dolphin kicks propelled me; my power in the water was undeniable. I felt like aqua woman. Or Wonder Woman. Better yet, with my hair streaming down my back, my legs and hips rocking together creating waves in the water, I was sexy. A temptress. Every man's image of slippery seduction: a mermaid.

Now for the magic.

My hands cupped the water and pushed it away from my body. The pull movement formed a perfect *S* beside my torso. My head popped up at the exact time my arms swung forward from underwater. Perfect arm extensions in combination motored by butterfly kicks created a fluid motion.

My chest pressed down, my hips went up and I purposefully

broke the water's surface in a seductive wave-like fashion.

Gorm positioned himself at the end of the pool. With each dip and rise he watched me. With each dip and rise, I moved more and more seductively toward him.

I've got him now. He's all mine.

My arms arched one last time before I reached the wall of the pool and made a two-handed touch. I looked up at him.

A mixture of admiration and respect reflected in his eyes.

"You really know what you're doing in there."

"Little bit." I raised my hand in the air to shield the afternoon sun that had shifted. My other hand hung onto the side of the pool.

Gorm stepped in front of me to block the glare. I smiled.

I had managed to jump in the pool without him seeing me in my high school Speedo. Now...

"Hey, why don't you get out and join us in the kiddie pool? James has something he wants to show you," Gorm said.

I'd love to, but there's the matter of me getting out of the water without you seeing me in this gawd awful suit. I tapped my teeth together. *Think. Think. Think.*

"What's on your mind?" Gorm knelt down in front of me.

"Nothing. What makes you think there is?"

"Well, for starters you look like you're about to have a panic attack or maybe you need to use the restroom? It's hard to tell."

"You're such a dork." I pushed off from the side of the pool and started treading water. "I'm not panicked and I *don't* need to use the ladies room."

My legs moved up and down in the deep end. *Maybe if I could get my thighs to look super tone then it won't be so bad.* I kicked up the speed and soon my movements no longer looked like treading water, but someone thrashing around in the water.

"Are you okay?"

I nodded and kept the rapid pace. My thighs burned and my arms were about to give out. *Damn it.*

I punched through the water with my hand and swam back to the edge of the pool.

"Look," I said trying to catch my breath. "I wanted to impress with you with my sick swimming skills and..." I held up a finger and shook it. "I think I did." I smacked the warm pool deck with my hand. Gorm jumped back a bit. "But enough's enough."

He placed his hand on mine. "Ohhh-kay. You did impress me. You're one helluva swimmer."

"I know. So..." I tilted my head. "Do you think you could turn around while I got out of the pool?"

Gorm shook his head. "Are you serious?"

"Yeah, you know, close your eyes, count to ten, ready or not..."

His baritone laugh rose out of him. "Is that what's got you so wound up?"

I splashed water on him. "Really? It's not so funny."

"Dani, I've seen your body."

I released my hand from his and wagged my finger. "No, I kept *my* clothes on." I now pointed toward him. "I've seen *your* body. And it's damn near perfect." I pressed my hand against my chest. "I on the other hand I've had three children. That's three," I raised three fingers in the air, "three times..." I wasn't sure where I was going with that statement. Of course, he knew I had three children. *Duh.*

"It's just really hard to feel or *look* sexy in a Speedo," I settled in the middle of insecurity and reality.

Gorm leaned toward me. I gripped the side of the pool with one hand and was ready to pull him in with the other.

"Dani, you're smokin'."

I rolled my eyes. "Gorm, I'm not. I'm a forty-something-year-old single mom with..."

"A killer body and great curves. You have an hourglass figure that most women would die for. It's not too much, it's not too little, it's just right."

I studied his eyes. They pooled in color.

"Hourglass, huh?"

"Oh, yeah and it's sexy as hell." A satisfied smirk crossed his face. "Dani, if your family wasn't here, I'd have you right now on the pool deck."

A faint smile curved my lips. We stared into each other's eyes.

"Thank you." I cupped my hand and moved the water around me in circles. "I'm still new at this."

Gorm gave another hearty chuckle. "Well, for a newcomer you sure know what you're doing."

I scooped water into the cup of my hand and tossed it at him. He inched away from being sprayed.

"Hey, I thought I was the one who's supposed to get you wet."

Heat tinged my cheeks. "You are so naughty."

"That's the only reason you're interested."

"You got me there." I placed both hands on the edge of the pool and rose up. Water slid down my body and for a moment I felt sexy. Then the wind kicked up.

I crossed my hands over my chest and cocked my head toward a lounge chair. "Can you get my towel?"

Gorm quickly returned and wrapped the towel around my shoulders. I already had goose bumps along my arms.

"Damn Wyoming wind cuts right through you." I rubbed the towel against my shoulders. Then I bent down and dried my legs.

When I stood Gorm's eyes roved over my body. They settled

on my breasts. "Doesn't leave much for the imagination, does it?"

I pulled the suit away from my body but the thin, wet nylon snapped back to hug my curves.

Gorm couldn't stop staring at me. It wasn't creepy or perverted. When Gorm looked at me it was the perfect balance between desire and reverence. I knew that if I put the brakes on things right now, he'd honor my request. *Chase never looked at me like this. Why did I settle for less than I deserve? When did I lose myself?*

Gorm stepped toward me. He placed his hands on my triceps. "Dani..." He shook his head. "I wish you could see yourself through my eyes."

Emotions lodged in my throat. I tried to swallow them down but I couldn't. His eyes held me. They were the same clear blue consistency of the water. And like the water I felt safe, secure and confident.

"If you could see what I see."

I leaned my cheek on his hand. "I'm beginning to." My eyes brimmed with tears and one fell on his hand. "Why are you so nice to me?"

His face softened. "It's easy."

I flicked away a tear and softly smiled. "Are you still drunk?" I half-laughed.

"Sober as a judge." He pulled me toward him and put his arms around me. I didn't know if my parents or my children could see us and in that moment I didn't care.

CHAPTER 14

"DANIELLA, DO you have a minute?"

I gritted my teeth. "Sure, Dad, just a second."

Damn it. What now? I had finally settled James down for a late nap. I secured a movie that both Michael and Josie agreed upon and set them up with a bowl of popcorn. Gorm had headed home from the pool to shower and change and I was about to dive into a trashy romance novel.

I folded down the corner of the book page and smiled. My father, the Professor, frowned upon this. *It ruins the preservation of the book. Blah. Blah. Blah.*

"Daniella?"

"On my way."

I hopped off the barstool at the breakfast bar and went to my father's library. I still hadn't retrieved the photo. I stole a glance at his desk. It wasn't lying on top so that was a good sign.

My father waited until I was inside the room before he pulled the barn doors closed behind us. He turned around with anger in his eyes and contempt in his voice. "I do not appreciate your public display with that man at the pool this afternoon."

"What?" *Is he talking about Gorm?* I stood and stared past my father and focused on the barn doors. I found a spot in the wood and keyed in on it.

"Daniella, the ink has barely dried on your divorce papers and you are already cavorting with someone."

I looked away from the door and at my father. "I thought you liked Gorm?"

"Gorm? Who's Gorm?" An empty vacant look crossed his face.

I shook my head. "Chris Gorham, your neighbor. What are *you* talking about?"

"I am discussing your behavior at the pool today." My father crossed his arms over his chest and hovered over me. "It was highly inappropriate and showed a gross lack of judgment. If you had shown just *one* ounce of interest in your career as you have with your love life you could have had a brilliant career."

I don't even know where to begin. I stood dazed. I felt emotion drain from my body replaced by numbness. *So you don't like Gorm? Or is it just me in general?*

"What do you have to say for yourself?" My father held his stance in front of his closed library doors. There was no way out, but past him. I wanted to switch my emotions to autopilot, but my father's visible contempt sparked a fire in my belly.

"I'm not *with* anyone and even if I were I really don't see how that, or my career, is any of your business."

My father's grey-blue eyes narrowed. "It certainly *is* my business."

"No," I stepped toward him. "It's not."

My father took an even, steady breath. "I would like to believe that's true, until this one falls apart and you show up on my doorstep."

His words stung and my throat tightened. I refused to let

him see me cry. I swallowed hard and stared into his unwavering eyes. It was a hollow abyss.

"I don't remember asking you to bail me out financially or emotionally from either of my marriages. I am temporarily staying here because Mom suggested it. *She* was there for me. You purposefully detached yourself from my life a long time ago. But, I guess I really shouldn't be surprised."

"What is that supposed to mean?" He uncrossed his arms and mounted them on his hips. I mirrored his move. We looked like a standoff in an old Western.

"Dad, you pride yourself so much on being a well-rounded man with your doctorate degree and varied awards. *Everyone* loves the professor and God knows you love the accolades." A cool, even stare settled on my face. "But I guess you didn't plan on children, correction, one of your children throwing a wrench into your perfectly planned life. When that happened, you made sure to be as far away from the debris as possible."

I took a breath to steady myself.

"Who I choose to spend time with is *my* business and none of your concern. My children and I will be out of your house as soon as possible."

My father's eyes suddenly looked empty. Still, I pushed past him toward the doors. He reached out and grabbed my shoulder. "Daniella."

I pulled away. "No, I'm over you looking down your nose at me. I think it's great that you found your soul mate and that your life with mom turned out to be just as you imagined."

I felt tears well in the corners of my eyes. I bit down hard on the inside of my cheek to stop the feeling from coming to the surface. I slid my hand between the barn doors to separate them and myself from my father.

I turned. "Dad, you're a brilliant success in every aspect

of your life." I looked at him. "Yet, you've failed miserably in compassion. When Chase left me for another woman, hell, left his son and our family, a phone call, a card, even an email would have been better than your icy silence. I get it. I screwed up—again. Got it. If distancing yourself from the black sheep of your family makes you feel better about yourself and your life then *bravo*. But don't come in and think for a second that you can play armchair quarterback with how I chose to live the second half of my life, when you weren't there for the first half."

I pulled the doors apart, but before I left I glared at my father. My pulse was pounding. "And don't feed me this bull last night about 'family' and being there for me when it's obvious you resent it when you do."

My steps were heavy when I walked away.

I found Gorm at the breakfast bar reading my book. "Saucy stuff." He shook the book toward me and I lightly chuckled.

"You okay?" he asked.

"Perfectly okay." I slammed my ass down in the barstool beside him.

He slowly nodded.

"I showed a little backbone with my Dad." My mouth twisted in a snare. "He was giving me hell about..." I gave a cursory glance at the library. The barn doors were closed. The Professor was probably stewing. *Good.*

"I heard a little of your conversation with your dad when your mom let me in."

I looked back at the hallway and suddenly remembered the picture I found after our late night rendezvous. It was still beneath my father's desk blotter. *Ah, what the hell. Let him find it. His precious XYZ fraternity might not be so precious after all.* I glared at the closed library doors.

"He was doing what I think dads of daughters do."

I turned back and looked at Gorm.

"He was being protective," he explained. "If I had a daughter, I'd have done the same thing."

"That's bullshit." I leaned toward Gorm and tapped my finger on his chest. "And you know it."

Gorm leaned against the back of the barstool. "No, it's not bull. It's what I would've have done if I saw a guy inappropriately hitting on my daughter at the local swimming pool."

I wanted to laugh, but the intensity in Gorm's eyes squelched the impulse.

"Dani, your dad cares deeply for you. He showed that when he was extremely considerate to both of us and asked to speak with you alone. He could have handled that a lot differently, but he didn't."

"Whose side are you on anyway?"

"This isn't about sides. There are some things that aren't up for competition."

The truth sank into the pit of my stomach. I looked down and brushed the hardwood floor with my painted toenail. "I'm just *so* tired of being judged."

Gorm tilted my chin up toward him. "I don't think that's what your Dad was doing."

I rolled my eyes. "Yeah, well, you didn't hear him."

"Men are stupid. We come off a little harsh when we're concerned about someone we love. We don't like feeling powerless."

Who are you? Why do you care? I bit my lower lip. "You think that's how my Dad felt? Powerless?"

His eyes softened. "I would bet money on it." Gorm inched forward in his seat and reached for my hand. "Dani, your dad adores you. He hangs on your every word. He doesn't want to see you get hurt. And right now, I'm the most likely candidate to do that."

You're not going to hurt me, are you? My eyes spoke the words that remained buried in my throat.

Gorm pulled me toward him and spoke into my hair. "Give it time. Your dad needs to see that I'm not like the other guys."

So do I.

CHAPTER 15

A BUCKET of fried chicken and cartons of mashed potatoes, gravy and coleslaw cluttered the kitchen counter. It was a food feast.

All that remained on my paper plate were bones and a butter stain from the heaping amount of taters I devoured. Comfort food did the one thing it was touted for: comfort. Though the bottle of wine that Gorm and I were drinking didn't hurt either.

I leaned next to Gorm and read over his shoulder. The romance novel I recently bought was providing some fun fodder.

My brother, Finn, found us at the kitchen bar. I held a page with my thumb and looked up.

"Hey! Come read this with us," I said. "Gorm was right. It's saucy."

"I heard you had a disagreement with dad," he said softly.

I rolled my eyes. "No, I just finally leveled the playing field and found my voice. I'm tired of his condescension toward me."

Finn gripped the kitchen counter and his eyes began to mist. "We need to talk about dad," he said and suddenly I no longer knew which way was up.

His words hung in the air: dementia, disorientated, Alzheimer's.

"When did this happen?" The barstool I sat on held my weight, but I still felt like I was falling. "Where have I been? Why didn't I see this?" A hollow, empty feeling settled over me.

I swallowed, but the lump in my throat remained. "Finn..." My voice was barely audible. "Will he even remember me?"

My brother reached across the kitchen counter and squeezed my hand. "Oh, Slim. Sweetie, I'm sorry. I *know* it's a lot to digest and we don't know the actual progression of dad's..." His voice cracked. He rapped his fingers on the counter trying to regain his composure.

Oh, Finn. Tears fell down my cheeks.

"How long have you known?" I asked softly.

He shrugged like he was trying to shake the weight of the world off his shoulders. "The doctors have run a lot of tests on dad, but nothing's definitive." Finn reached across the kitchen counter and refilled my wine glass.

"Dementia." I shook my head. "It just doesn't seem right. It's the *one* title that doesn't belong to our father."

"I'm sorry you're going through this," Gorm said to both of us.

"You knew," I stated rather than asked.

Finn nodded. "Gorm's been an incredible help to Mom. Dad's locked himself out of the house so many times, without Gorm, I think Mom would have lost it a long time ago."

"Why didn't you tell me?" I looked at Gorm.

"I asked him not to," Finn said.

I stared at my brother. He looked so much like our father that it was a painful reminder of the younger dad who had risen to such great heights and now barely remembered my children's names. And like our father he was now taking the lead in the family.

I turned toward Gorm. "Thank you for..." I shrugged. "Everything."

His eyes warmed back at me. "It was the least I could do. Your father is a great guy."

We all took a sip of wine. The merlot flowed freely, but our spirits didn't. The fate of our father hung in the air like a storm cloud waiting to release a deluge.

"Fried chicken and red wine...don't get that every day," Finn said though his voice didn't carry the lightness he had intended.

"Or news of your father's declining mental health," I said and wished I hadn't.

Gorm raised his glass. "I'd like to propose..."

I shook my head. *What?* I extended my glass toward his and my brother met us in the center.

"A pledge," Gorm said.

Finn and I nodded in unison.

"A pledge that no matter how much life throws at us, with aging or absent parents," Gorm paused and rubbed the rough stubble on his chin with his free hand. For a moment, he was somewhere else. Then he cleared his throat and continued, "no matter what happens," he raised his glass high in the air, "this is our pledge to be there for each other."

My brother lightly touched Gorm's glass against his. Deep, dark, rich red wine whirled in little waves as we collided our goblets together.

"I'd better check on my wife," Finn said. "I left Melissa downstairs with the kids and a glass of wine. I'm sure that's too much of one and not enough of the other." Finn disappeared from the kitchen.

I turned toward Gorm. "Thank you for being here – again."

He gently smiled. "I wouldn't want to be anywhere else."

"So what'd you mean by absent? And earlier you said something about..." My mind went blank. *Great. I'm turning into my father.* I suppressed the urge to giggle at the depressing and mildly sad thought. *Am I bad person for having mixed emotions about all of this?* I quickly shook my head. My recall was foggy. "Oh...you said something earlier about parents. Or you inferred to them."

Gorm swirled his wine. Merlot banked off the inside of the glass. The legs of the wine slowly crept down the sides. It was a tangy vintage and made my mouth pucker. I glanced at the empty bottle. I was beginning to feel its effects.

"Don't you remember?" I pinched my lips together and waited for the aftertaste to subside. "You made some comment about tricky father stuff, but that I had the chance to make it right. What'd ya mean by that?"

Gorm's blue eyes darkened and took on a stormy, overcast look. "I also said I don't like secrets."

"Uh-huh, me neither, so I don't understand."

"That makes two of us." Gorm stopped swirling his wine and took a long, deep drink. He pushed back the barstool he sat on and stood up. He held his hand out toward me. "Come on. We haven't seen your dad in a while. We should go check on him."

I took his hand and suddenly began to laugh.

"What's so damn funny?"

"Well, when we find the Professor we *best* not be holding hands or I'll get another talkin' too about how inappropriate we are."

Gorm smiled with a wink. "But I like to be inappropriate."

Well, okay then. I can get on board with that.

Gorm elbowed me. "How 'bout it? Right here by the kitchen."

I swatted his shoulder. "Good try. You're such a Boy Scout you'd never do something that risky. I'm the trouble maker."

"We'll see." Gorm gently dropped my hand to pick up his wine glass. He threw back the rest of his Merlot. "Now," he left the empty glass on the bar, "let's find the Professor before we both end up in trouble."

We found my father in the library.

"This is like *Clue*," I said when we opened the barn doors.

My father's black leather executive chair was turned toward the bookshelf, but his tanned arm was visible on the armrest. His fraternity ring shone in the late setting sun. I wondered if Gorm noticed it. *Doubt it.* He seemed too preoccupied as we entered my father's sanctuary.

I lowered my voice. "It was the Professor with the candlestick in the library." I giggled. Despite a belly full of comfort food, the wine had a better hold of my senses.

Gorm put his finger up to his mouth. "Shhh."

This only made me laugh more.

Gorm's eyebrows furrowed and he got seriously beady-eyed.

"Don't shush me." I tried to lightly tap him on the back, but missed. *I have horrible depth perception when I drink.*

Gorm shot me a frustrated look. *He's worried about my dad. Or is there more to it?* Still his concern and the recent revelation about my father's possible deteriorating mental health sobered me. *There's really nothing funny about this.* I knew the humor was merely masking my hurt.

"Hey." This time I made contact with Gorm. "Could I have a minute with my dad?"

He nodded and spoke quietly. "I'll let Finn know we found him."

I closed the barn doors behind Gorm and latched them in place. I was either keeping my father locked in with me or my family locked out from disturbing us. I wasn't sure.

My father remained steadfast in his chair.

This is going to be harder than I thought. I walked toward his desk and stopped mid-way. *He feels powerless.* Gorm's insight suddenly overrode my ego and the anesthetizing effect of the wine.

"Dad." My voice sounded small. I stood a foot from the edge of my father's desk with my hands interlaced. "I'm sorry." It felt like an act of contrition. All that was missing was my rosary.

The chair remained locked in place. The high back faced me in a grand gesture of screw you.

I waited for my father to respond. *Say something. Anything. Yell at me. Geez. Just get it over with.*

The longer my father remained silent, the more his hurt became tangible. I walked softly toward the chair. I peered around it.

"Dad?" His eyes were closed and his head was tilted to the side. He had fallen asleep. All the fight was erased from his face. I leaned over and gently kissed his cheek.

"I'm sorry," I whispered.

The scent of his aftershave rose to my nose. It was strong, spicy and practically made my eyes water. It was vintage dad cologne.

I looked over my shoulder at the window seat. One of my grandmother's crocheted afghans was folded neatly in the corner. I grabbed it and was about to lay the brown and green horizontal-stripped blanket on my father when I noticed the black and white photograph in his lap. He held it tightly in his left hand. I tucked the afghan under my arm and gingerly tugged on the photo when my father's grey-blue eyes snapped open.

"Jesus!" I jumped. The afghan fell to the floor.

Startled, my father jerked back in his chair. He gripped the photo against his chest.

Shit.

His eyes widened and he quickly surveyed the room.

He's disorientated. No wonder why Mom didn't want the kids to ever wake him up. He looks scared.

I knelt in front of my larger-than-life father who suddenly looked dwarfed by his chair. His eyes were misty and his jaw was clenched. He gripped the picture like a life preserver. The back of the photo was facing me. A date was stamped in the center of the paper. I tilted my head and read the black lettering: April 17, 1964. *I was born in 1969.*

"Daniella?" His voice was husky, almost hoarse.

I looked up at my father. *He doesn't remember our fight.* Words were stuck in my throat. I nodded.

"Darling, what are you doing here?"

Dad? My heart sank in my chest. *Is that really you?*

"Daniella, honey, what's going on?"

For a brief moment I smiled. *This is the father that loves me. This is my dad. This isn't the lofty Professor.* I lowered my head and discreetly wiped my eyes. I looked up and placed my hand on his knee. "Dad, the kids and I are here because I start my new job tomorrow, remember?"

"That's right, that's right." Suddenly his response sounded rehearsed.

My stomach began to rattle and I knew I was moments away from breaking down. *Don't. Don't do that to him. Keep it together, Dani. Do this for Dad. This is how to apologize.* I clapped my hands together. The sound was jarring to both of us.

"Well, I better go get my notes organized for tomorrow's class." I didn't move from my stance in front of my father. I didn't know how to leave. *I may not see this dad again. It'd already been years since this kinder, softer dad had been present.* I gently bowed my head. Tears fell from my face. I couldn't stop them. I bit my lip to keep it from trembling. My shoulders shook. I was a mess.

I felt my father's hand on my head. "Daniella."

I nodded.

"Look at me."

I lifted my head. His hand cupped my chin.

"You've got your father's Irish temper, don't you love?"

My face crumbled and I lowered my head on his knee. "Dad, I'm sorry. I am *so* sorry."

"Shh, shh, now. It's over. We both said some awful things, didn't we?"

I couldn't swallow. *He did remember. I don't know if that makes it better or worse.* I tapped my forehead against his knee. "I didn't mean it. I was..."

"Daniella, you and I are very much alike."

I looked up at him. "I'm not. I wish I was more like you, then I'd be... well, then you'd be...proud of me." I put my hand over my mouth to quiet the hurt that threatened to choke me if I let it all come out.

"Oh." He put the photo on his desk. A younger version of my father smiled at me. The older version leaned forward in his chair and rested his forehead against mine. "I *am* proud of you."

I shook my head against my father's. "No, it's okay. I've made a lot of mistakes." I pulled away from him and wiped my eyes. "But I'm getting back on my feet. I am."

My father reached for my hands and held them. "Do you know it took me *years* to get back on my feet when the love of my life left me?"

"What?" *Did I just hear that correctly?* "What are you talking about?"

He tilted his head toward his desk. "That photo. I came across it today and..."

Oh crap. What do I say? How do I explain this?

My father's eyes got misty.

Maybe there's nothing *to say.*

He let go of one of my hands and pinched his eyelids together. When he opened them he looked right at me. "Your mom wasn't my first love. The *great plan* you said that I had for my life... well, she fell in love with my best friend."

He stared at the picture. "It took me years to get over that."

"But you married Mom in 1965? You had Fiona in 1966. The picture is from 1964." *That doesn't make sense.*

He slowly nodded. "I was and I *am* in love with your mother. She saved me. She still does...*every* day. But it took me a long time to find my footing again. I lost Vivian and my best friend."

Vivian. "Is that the woman in the picture?"

My father smiled. "Daniella, there are four women in that picture."

"But you're only smiling at one."

A single tear ran down my father's face. "Everyone loves a lover, and you child, are a lover. Oh, Daniella, you make me smile with your heart." He shook his head. "It was a lifetime ago." He exhaled a long breath. "Vivian's heart belonged to Andrew. She only had eyes for him."

Andrew. "He's the man standing behind her?"

He nodded. "He adored her. He followed her in a room with his eyes. Hell, we all did." A wry chuckle rose from his soft voice. "She was our Homecoming Queen and the queen of many hearts. There are just some women like that. Their energy and grace are what men fall in love with."

He lightly tapped the end of my nose. "Daniella, men fall in love with women like Vivian because of who they feel like they could *be* when they're with her."

He cradled my face in his hands. "Mike and Chase fell in love with who they saw when they looked in your eyes. Daniella, don't you see that you make people feel alive and loved? They feel cherished. When those men left it's because of who *they* were. It had *nothing* to do with you. They couldn't stand the thought of disappointing you so before you could find out that they weren't quite up to snuff, they left."

My tears collected in my father's hands.

"They tried to make it seem like it was about you, that it was *your* fault, but it wasn't."

"Do you mean that?" My voice was so tender and raw it was barely recognizable.

My father tilted my face toward him and kissed my forehead. "I saw it happen with Vivian when Andrew left. He just disappeared. Vivian was left to pick up the pieces of her life and wonder what she had done for him to leave."

I felt my heart begin to race. "What happened to her?" *What will happen to me?*

"She moved away, got married and had a little boy."

He gently tapped the table in the photo.

"That was the last night I saw Andrew. Vivian fell apart after that." My father held his hand over his mouth and exhaled. He picked up the photo. "I heard she moved back to Casper and brought a ranch just outside of town, but I haven't seen her. I don't even know her married name."

I nodded trying desperately to absorb everything he was telling me.

"To my knowledge, Vivian only suffered one serious heartbreak and that was Andrew. And in turn," he laid the photo back on his desk, "mine was Vivian."

I stared at my father until his face began to blur. I rubbed my eyes.

"Daniella, one heartbreak is enough for a lifetime. I *know*. To have my daughter have to endure it twice, well…" He shook his head. "It's too much to bear. I worry about you. I don't want..."

"To see me get hurt again?" *Neither does Gorm.*

He nodded. "I know you're strong, but why put yourself through that again?"

A humorless laugh escaped my lips. "I guess I'm hoping the third time's the charm."

A gentle smile filled his face. "You know the luck of the Irish is usually for those that don't have it?"

"I know." I stood up and grabbed the afghan off the floor. I shook it out and folded it back into a square. I held it against my chest and looked at my father.

"You're as stubborn as your mother," he said.

"And I lead with my heart like my father."

CHAPTER 16

"EVERYONE SAY their goodbyes to Finnegan. His plane leaves early tomorrow morning." My mother's voice found its way into the library. "And Michael leaves for football camp."

"Better shake a leg. I don't want your mother scolding us." My father stood from his chair and straightened his polo shirt and wiped his eyes. "How do I look?"

I didn't expect my reaction. But when my father looked over at me I lowered my head and felt a tear roll down my cheek.

"That bad, huh?"

I looked up and started to laugh. "Who are you and what did you do with my dad?"

He fanned the air between us with his hand. "Ah, that's nonsense."

I don't have a poker face and it showed in my reaction.

He stepped toward me and put his hands on the outside of my shoulders. "Some days, Daniella, are better than others."

"Fair enough." I pointed toward the barn doors. "Let's go find the troops."

Gorm was with the kids at the kitchen table. He dished out

dessert. *Why couldn't my dad see this?* I looked around, but he had suddenly vanished. *Great! He only gets to see Gorm grope me.*

"I'm sorry." I said out of habit. "You shouldn't be doing that."

Gorm shrugged. "It's fun. I haven't had little people around in a long time." He passed out the last plate of ice cream cake and then pushed himself away from the table. "I should be going. I've already worn out my welcome."

I shook my head. "No, don't leave."

"I have a ton of work to catch up on." He reached over and patted James on the back. "Hey buddy, you did great in the pool today. I was really impressed."

My son looked up at him and beamed. "Thanks, Goldfish."

"It's Gorm!" I said with a chuckle.

James giggled. "Thanks *Gorm*."

Michael cocked his head toward Gorm. "Hey, thanks for hanging out with us. That was pretty cool."

Peace fell over me as I watched how easily my boys interacted with Gorm. This man seemed to meld right into my broken family.

Gorm smiled. "Anytime guys. Thanks for letting me join you." He extended his closed knuckles toward Michael. "Hey, good luck at football camp tomorrow. You're going to do great."

Michael smiled.

I walked Gorm to the front door when he saw Finn in the library.

"Would you mind if I," he nudged his head toward the library. "I'd like to say my goodbyes to your brother. I'll see myself out after that."

"Sure, that's fine. Is everything okay?" I hated the insecurity I heard in my voice, but it was nonetheless there.

"Things couldn't be better," he said, yielding a crooked

smile. He looked around the hallway and then cautiously kissed me on the cheek. *What does a girl gotta do around here to get more than a motherly peck?*

"Wow. That'll keep me warm tonight," I said.

His cheeks reddened. "It's the best I can do considering..." I felt the heat of his eyes on me. "I'd like to do more."

I'd like for you to do much, much, much more. I mischievously smiled at him.

"You start teaching tomorrow, right?"

I bit the side of my lip trying to act as seductively as I could.

Gorm put his hand on my hip and tilted his head toward mine. I moved into him. My body stirred with excitement. He bypassed my lips and whispered in my ear, "I'm hot for the teacher."

I punched him in the upper arm. "Go say your goodbyes to my brother."

CHAPTER 17

No AMOUNT of make up or eye cream could conceal my puffy eyes. I had expected an emotional goodbye with Michael, but not my brother.

Michael decided to stay overnight in the hotel with Finn and his family. By now, my brother had probably dropped Michael off at the high school and was headed to the airport.

Between Finn's farewell last night and my father's admission of his first love, I woke up with droopy, bloodshot eyes.

"Lovely." *Great way to start my first day of teaching. Wonderful.* I made one last sweep across my eyelids with the makeup brush and turned off the bathroom light.

Josie started to stir. Her petite torso was fanned across the bed with blankets in a disheveled mess beside her. I softly touched her ankle.

"Baby girl, I'm leaving now. Be good for Grandma and Grandpa. Love you."

Face down on a stack of pillows Josie barely raised her head. "Okay, have a good day. Love you, too."

I watched her drift back to sleep and pulled a blanket over

her. Despite my parents' aim to have a futuristic, modern home, cold air seemed to settle in their house like a drafty old Wyoming homestead. Mornings and evenings were the worst. I crossed my arms over my chest and rubbed them for warmth.

I saw James at the bottom of the stairs. He looked up as I bounded down.

"Momma, Momma, Momma! You won't guess what?"

I sat down next to him on the bottom step and pulled him onto my lap. I wrapped my arms around him and squeezed. He squirmed out from beneath my arms and stood stoically in front of me.

"Listen." His voice was serious and his eyes drew me in.

"I'm sorry." I quickly checked my watch. I still had ample time to get to campus before my first class started. "Okay," I put my hands on my knees. "What won't I guess?"

He leaned toward me. "I spied on Goldeneye."

"What?"

"Goldeneye. You know, who went to the pool with us."

"Gorm. It's Gorham or Gorm, not Goldeneye or gold-anything."

"Oh." James took a moment to enunciate the word. His mouth opened wide. "*Gorm.*"

I nodded with a smile.

"Well, I spied on him." James tilted his chin up, his expression clearly one of pride.

I took my hands off my knees and massaged the back of my neck. "Uh, I don't understand. When did you spy on him?"

A smug grin crossed my five-year-old's face. "After my nap."

Nap time. It was short-lived, but he did nap yesterday after the pool.

"I was laying down in the living room and then I saw Gorm in Grandpa's library so I spied on him."

I glanced at the two rooms. The living room was off to my right and my father's library was directly across the hallway. The staircase was the center divide between the two rooms.

I swept hair off of James' forehead. "What do you mean? How were you spying on Gorm?"

"I got off the couch and looked into Grandpa's library. I saw Gorm, and when he walked into Grandpa's library I hid down and watched him get his stuff."

"What stuff did he get?"

"Some paper on Grandpa's desk."

"Paper? Was Grandpa with him?"

"No. He was alone." His voice grew loud with excitement. "And he *stole* it."

"Oh, honey, that's..." I shook my head. "I don't think Gorm would have stolen anything."

James' eyes widened. "He did! I saw him." James pointed to the library. "He took the paper with all the people on it and put it in his shorts."

"The photo? Was it a photo?"

James raised his shoulders. "Dunno. Maybe."

"You said it had people on it."

"Yeah, boys and girls at a table."

I kneaded my forehead. "Are you sure?"

James moved his head up and down. "Yup."

"How did you see this again?"

"I used my *spy periscope*." My son's voice took on a sharp edge.

If I tick him off, he'll shut down and I won't get any answers. I contemplated my next move when James shook his hands in the air in aggravation.

"Spy periscope."

"Baby," my voice was earnest, "I don't know what that is."

James ran into the living room and returned with what looked like a miniature periscope.

"Is this what your dad got you before we left? Was this your goodbye gift?"

"Yup. He got me a bunch of spy gear. Cool, huh?"

I forced a smile. *Wonderful. Great. Swell Chase.*

"Wasn't that so nice of my dad?"

I grinned until it hurt.

Ironic too. Why the hell is that no-good, lying, cheatin', bastard of an ex-husband, giving our son spy gear? Does he expect James to spy on me? I felt my heart race and I wanted to break the periscope in half, but instead I took a calm steady breath and watched my animated son explain the fundamentals of spy gear.

"See, there's a little black thing here," he pointed to the eyepiece. "Its rubber and you put your eye on it. And there's a little mirror inside at the top and at the bottom. The mirrors do something like flash up and down and the picture comes back to where my eye is. So I can move it and I can turn it up. When I turn it up, the mirror goes up and I can see around corners."

"Really?"

James proudly smiled and handed it to me. "You can see in front of you and behind you."

I looked into the eyepiece and depending on where I turned the scope, I could clearly see into the living room, library or up the stairs. *That's pretty cool.* I adjusted the scope toward my father's library. His desk was in full view and it was completely clear of any paper or photo. It was pristine.

"Huh." My eye pressed into the periscope. "And you can see around corners, too?"

James smiled. "Yup."

"That's how you saw Gorm in Grandpa's library with this

thing?" I removed it from my eye and handed it back to James. "You saw it all with this spy periscope."

James looked longingly at his spy gear and then at me. "I saw him take that paper off of Grandpa's desk. I didn't know if I should grab a book and hit him over the head and dial nine-one-one."

I choked down a giggle. "No, no, we don't need to dial nine-one-one. Only in emergencies."

"But he was *stealing* from Grandpa!"

I gently touched my son's cheek. "I'm sure Gorm was simply *borrowing* something from Grandpa."

James considered my answer and then moved to the next subject. "I have another spy gear that you can take pictures with. It's red and you can take pictures in the dark."

Very cool. I could have used a camera like that the other night when we found that ring with the bones. "Will you show it to me?"

"Okay, you go to Grandpa's library and I'll be right there." James scurried off and I followed his orders. I walked into the library and stood by my father's desk. I lifted up the desk blotter. *Maybe the photo got tucked underneath. Nope.* There wasn't anything under his desk blotter, not even dust. *Mom's got way too much time on her hands.*

From across the hallway, James waved me closer toward the desk.

"Gorm was standing with his back to Grandpa's big window," he said.

I took my son's stage directions and mirrored Gorm's last known movements in the library "Right there." James held his hand up. "Perfect."

James aimed a long, rectangular-shaped, sleek black box at me. He paused and then held the gismo out in front of him.

"Alright!" He raised his hand up in the air and then ran across the hallway, into the library and to my father's desk. His head barely touched the top of it.

"See!" He showed me the spy device. It was a miniature camera that took infrared photos. James pressed a button and a black-and-white image of me in the library surfaced on the small screen. It had a dreamlike quality to it. The ceiling in the library was very dark and the area around me was somewhat hazy, but aside from a few shadows and dark reflections off the desk, there was no mistaking me in the picture.

"Did you take a picture of Gorm?"

James shook his head. "No because Gorm looked around and I thought he saw me so I hid behind the couch."

"*Did* he see you?"

"No."

"How do you know?"

"Because he would have said something to me if he had."

Sometimes my son's logic was sounder than mine.

"Gorm didn't spot me. I spotted him. He took the paper and tucked it in the back of his shorts and pulled his shirt over it."

"He hid it in his shorts?" The tone of my voice peeked.

James nodded. "Yup, like this." My son took a piece of paper from the paper tray from my father's printer and slipped it into the back of his waistband. He pulled his shirt over his shorts and started to walk out of the library.

"Unbelievable."

James turned back around. "Is Grandpa going to be mad at him?" Serious grey-blue eyes looked at me.

I quickly shook my head. "No, no."

"I got up a few minutes after Gorm left and went to tell you. I came up to your room, but you were hugging Uncle Finn and then I forgot."

I nodded. *Maybe Dad put the picture back in the album.* I knelt down and pulled open the window drawer where I had found the picture. I pulled out the top album and flipped through the pages. Nothing was loose or stuffed in between the pages. *Damn it. I wanted to take the picture with me to work today and show Ruth.* I scrolled to the back of the album and found the page where the picture had been. All that remained were four black photo corners. *What the hell?* I put the album back and rolled the drawer closed.

I held James' spy camera. "So you didn't get any pictures of Gorm?"

"I did, but it's not very good because I was hiding by the couch."

My heart started beating faster. "Can I see what you took?"

I handed the camera to my son. He pressed on a button. Images blurred past him. "There it is!" He handed me the camera.

The photo had more of a milky look to it and reminded me of a negative image more than an actual image. Despite the grainy image, it still clearly showed Gorm holding what appeared to be my father's photo in his hand. *Not very incriminating, but why take it?*

CHAPTER 18

"GOOD MORNING and welcome to *Researching Facts for Fiction*. I'm Dani Quinn and I'll be instructing this class for the next eight weeks."

The classroom was half-full, which was markedly better than half-empty. *Ah, Gorm's having a positive effect on me.* The students sat quietly while my mind played tug of war with my emotions. *Focus Dani. Gorm may not be such a good guy after all. I still don't know if he took that picture. Or why.*

I diverted the questioning stares from my students and reached into my briefcase, withdrawing the vanilla-colored file folder that Ruth prepared. *Where has she been all my life?* I smiled to myself and pulled out the first of three paper clipped set of handouts.

I unclipped the first stack, kept the top copy and handed a set of introduction sheets to an elderly gentleman. "Please take one and pass it back."

In fact, when I quickly scanned the faces, I realized that the majority of the class was comprised of what educators classified as older adult learners. *Huh.* My mind quickly recalled the three

categories of learners in adult education. The younger adults are
those who are in their teens to mid-twenties, and then there are
the working adults who are in their upper-twenties to retirement
age. And anyone sixty-five or older are the older adult learners. I
looked at the warm faces that were smiling at me.

Yup. I've got the seniors.

The man in the front row raised his hand.

I smiled. Younger adults rarely raise a hand. They tended
to be the "burst-out-an-answer" type. This was a rather nice
change.

"Since I haven't taken roll yet," I said. "It's usually not
required in a non-credited course, but I'd really like to get to
know each of you. So before you ask your question, would you
please introduce yourself?"

"Richard, but please call me 'Dick.'"

I gritted a smile. *Do I have to?*

"Quinn...are you Joe Quinn's daughter?"

I tensely grinned. *And here we go with the famous pedigree.*
"Yes, I am."

"Well, he's a good man. We went to college together."

I relaxed my jaw and looked at his hands interlaced on the
desk in front of him. No visible fraternity ring.

"Um, Miss Quinn?"

I resumed eye contact with Richard.

"We were told this was more of a genealogy class."

"Huh." I slowly nodded. *Genealogy, family trees, so not
what I have prepared.* "Well..." I glanced at my pile of handouts
that were geared toward the importance and value of research in
a work of fiction. I scratched my forehead. *If they drop the class,
I don't get paid.*

I clapped my hands together. This seemed to have the same
reaction it did with my father. Everyone jumped.

"Okay, if it's genealogy you want, it's genealogy you'll get. After all," I said in a complete adlib, "the strategies for researching facts for fiction aptly apply to any form of research. So I'll tell you what in an effort to save paper..."

They were all seated around each other in a cluster. *Why do people do that? The entire classroom is open and they all gather in one area.*

"What I'd like you to do is to add the word *non* to wherever you see fiction." I smiled at the band of bona fide AARP'ers and passed out the next set of handouts.

Collectively they bobbed their heads. They looked like a school of hungry fish. While they went through two pages of handouts, I tried to access the Internet on my cell phone. I was going to Google genealogy, but the reception in the classroom was lousy. I slightly raised my voice. "When you're finished adding non in front of fiction, we'll take a five minute..." I looked at the seniors. "Ten minute restroom break."

A literal sense of relief washed over them. I glanced at the clock mounted on the wall behind me. "So let's return by ten after ten."

They nodded.

I casually walked out of the classroom and darted toward Ruth's office. I wasn't in platform sandals, but my wedged heels weren't any kinder to my feet. *Genealogy. Crap. What do I know about genealogy? Zip. Nada. Nothing.*

Ruth's fingers were quietly drumming the keyboard on her computer. Her fingers moved at light speed, but there wasn't any clanking of the keys.

"Look at you, Ms. Speedy Pants."

Her eyes twinkled along with her smile. "I used to teach typing, you know."

"No, I didn't or that you were a Canuck."

She smiled. "I'm from *South* Dakota—Armour, South Dakota to be exact."

I lightly chuckled. "Ohh-kay. And that little accent?"

Ruth fanned the air. "Ah, the accent thingy is talking like the Norwegians that are from North Dakota and Minnesota. Have you ever heard any of the Ole and Lena jokes?"

"Have to say thankfully I haven't." Being around Ruth was just fun. It made me completely forget about the seniors waiting for me.

"Well, South Dakota has many Germans but the farther north—closer to North Dakota, there are more Pennsylvania Dutch and Norwegians."

She paused for a breath and I considered trading places with her. *Since she knows so much about geography and the history of the culture, she should teach this class, and I should type memos. I've made a huge mistake.*

"South Dakotans," she said, "have always made jokes about the Nodaks and Minniesoootans and their funny way of talking. Yeah sure, you betcha!"

The tension in my shoulders lessened.

Ruth grinned. "In South Dakota we drink pop, not soda and we eat at taverns instead of what you'd call a Sloppy Joe."

I tried so hard not to smile, but I couldn't help it. "You are *such* a dork."

Ruth leaned back in her executive chair and crossed her arms over her chest. "You left your class to come tell me this?"

"Oh, right!" I snapped my fingers. "I've got seniors. And lots of them."

Ruth nodded.

"*You're* not surprised." I moved toward her desk and sat down in the chair beside it.

"Your class is a non-credited course so anyone in the

community can enroll." Her grayish-green eyes looked at me from over the top of her glasses.

"And that's fine." I rapped my fingers on her desk. "My main concern is that they thought it was a *genealogy* course."

Ruth rolled her chair toward me. "Okay, so what's the problem?"

"Guess I'm having a senior moment." I chuckled. Ruth didn't.

"You know I'm sixty two, don't you?"

"Nope." I rubbed the back of my neck. "Not the adult learner category I would have placed you in."

Ruth smiled brightly. "Well, thank you."

Whew. Way to side step my unintended insult with an intended compliment. I grinned. "I'm just feeling a bit underprepared." *Something the Professor would completely frown upon.*

Ruth gently placed her hand over mine and stopped me from rapping against her shiny, streak-free desk.

"Sorry I'm kind of rambling and kind of messing up your desk." My jaw muscles clenched.

"Dani, you're going to do fine. Older adult learners are not much different than the students you've taught before."

"I know." With my free hand, I echoed one of my father's mannerisms and pinched my eyelids together. It instantly relieved the tension in my forehead. *Maybe the old man's onto something.*

When I opened my eyes, Ruth was smiling at me.

"Get back to your class and do what you do best."

"And that is?" I started to laugh.

"Dani, you're a positive, vibrant, energetic woman. Be yourself. Those old goats will love ya."

I rolled my eyes. "We'll see." I stood up, straightened my

blouse and checked the crease on my slacks. *Oh my God, I'm turning into the Professor*.

"I'll come check on you in a bit, though..." Ruth's voice wavered. "It may take me a while to get to your classroom."

I looked at her with concern. "Are you okay?"

"It's just that seniors, like myself, take a while to get around, you know."

I grinned. "Cute." I turned to leave.

"Hey, I meant to ask you, did you find anything out about the thing we discussed the other night."

I pivoted on the heel of my pump. "Actually, I found a picture."

Ruth's eyes widened.

"Yeah, well, that's the thing. I found it and then I lost it." *Or Gorm stole it.*

Ruth shook her head. "That doesn't sound like you."

"You're right." I exhaled a shallow breath. "It doesn't."

* * *

"Breaks over." I waited for the seniors to return to their seats. I sat on the corner of the desk in front of my first class and crossed my legs. The silver bracelet around my ankle shone in the morning light that flooded the room. I kicked my ankle back and forth. The silver roped anklet looked like a chain and reminded me of my father's favorite author, Charles Dickens and one of his favorite stories.

I can't remember my kids' names, but I can remember obtuse lines from literature. Go figure. A sudden rush of relief washed over me.

"I'm sure you are all familiar with Dickens," I began. *Now if I don't put them to sleep.*

Richard raised his hand.

I nodded toward him.

"Charles Dickens, the writer?"

"Yes." I just couldn't call him 'Dick.' "That's correct."

He beamed with pride.

"Charles Dickens was an English writer, who is probably most famous for his novella, *A Christmas Carol*."

A thin, petite woman with beautiful platinum hair held back by a simple black headband smiled. I returned the gesture. *She looks so familiar.*

"In the story," I continued, "Ebenezer Scrooge is visited by the Ghosts of Christmases Past, Present, and Yet to Come. In classic Dickens' style, we're going to visit the past."

I waited for a reaction. There was a general consensus of doubt on the faces of the adults.

"What I know for sure is that there are as many ways to begin your story as there are stories to be told. So whether you choose to prepare a genealogical history of your family or delve into telling *your* life story, there isn't one set start. That's the beauty of writing – whether it's fiction or nonfiction. It's *your* story. You're the writer. You set the tone."

The woman behind Richard nodded.

Inclusive learning. Engage the learners. Suddenly the first and only graduate course I completed before taking a maternity medical leave with Michael started filtering through my memory bank. *Older adults need to be active in their learning.*

"Miss?" I tilted my head toward the woman.

"Jean." A thick, Southern accent rolled off her tongue like sweet honey. "Gorham. Jean Gorham."

Did she just say Gorham? I reached for the class roster and scanned the alphabet. There was no Gorham listed.

"I'm sorry, Jean, were you a late enrollee?"

Her hair shook from side-to-side. "No, ma'am."

"I don't have a Gorham on my roster. Gorham *is* what you said, isn't it?" My stomach twisted. "Or did I misunderstand?" *Please let it be a mistake. Please. Please. Please.*

"No, ma'am, it's Gorham. Jean Gorham."

A sour taste seeped to the back of my throat and I began to sweat. My neck itched and I swear I felt the onset of hives. *Great, now I'm going to look like Typhoid Dani. Or worse, like one of Ebenezer's gruesome ghosts. If this is Gorm's mom, I'm making a horrible first impression.*

I wiped my forehead and squinted at the roster. I still could not find Gorham anywhere on the paper I looked up at her. If she was Gorm's mom, I couldn't see much of a resemblance. But then again, Gorm was bald and built like a defensive lineman and she didn't have any of these traits.

"Oh, dear," she said softly. "I bet it's under my maiden name."

I nodded. "And that would be..."

"Wilson."

My finger scrolled down the sheet and stopped at the bottom.

"Okay, I think I found you, but it shows a V.J. Wilson, is that you?"

Her gentile composure never changed. "Yes ma'am. Vivian Jean Wilson."

I put my hand to my chest. *Now I'm having a heart attack.* I cleared my throat, but it didn't prevent my voice from cracking. "Did you say Vivian?"

Her eyes were older, but the same sadness still engulfed them. *Oh my God!*

"Oh," she waved the air in front of her. "That's an awful name. My momma loved *Gone With The Wind*. I haven't gone by Vivian in years. Decades."

"Not since we were in college." Richard turned in his seat and looked at her. "Viv here was our Homecoming Queen and all around beauty."

"And Queen of Courts, remember?" another woman said. The rest of the class vouched for her with nods.

Oh my God. They all went to school together. They all know...my dad and...Vivian.

If I weren't already sitting down, my knees would have given out. As it was, I felt weak and the roster sheet shook in my hand. I set it back down on the desk. *Oh my God. This is my Dad's Vivian. This is the love of his life. But why does she have Gorm's last name?*

"Oh, Richard you're a dear man."

See, no one likes to call a man 'Dick.'

Richard blushed.

"Miss Quinn, I'm sorry to have caused such a fuss. I blame my sweet husband, Charles. When I met him, he called me by my middle name, Jean, and it just stuck. I don't even think my son knows my baptismal name."

"Son?" I felt my stomach do a summersault.

She smiled brightly. "Yes, love of my life, my sweet Christopher."

I literally gasped and quickly covered my mouth with my hand. *Oh no.* Everyone in the classroom stared at me. I swallowed the rising stomach acid and prayed a quick Hail Mary.

I inhaled deeply through my nose and slowly released the breath. *I got this. She doesn't know the naughty thing I did to her son or what my father told me about her.* I smiled.

"Well, Jean, I took us off on this tangent, and I do apologize." My hands moved wildly in the air with no rhythm or reason. It looked like I was about to start a revival and not finish teaching a class on a subject I knew nothing about. I put my hands on the desk and pressed them into the faux grain finish.

"Jean, it looked like you wanted to add something to the conversation, which was about writing and how it related to genealogy."

Her Bonnie-blue eyes gently acknowledged me. "You already answered my question. I was wondering if there was going to be a set of instructions for how to begin this, but it seems as though we get to make that choice ourselves."

"That's correct, Jean. Everyone gets to decide how to approach this." *Just like I get to decide how to approach this humdinger of a mess.*

"I'm hoping," I said, "that each of you will begin the writing process the way *you* envisioned it to be." I rubbed my forehead. *Stay on track.*

"The reason I'm choosing *A Christmas Carol* as an example for this assignment is twofold." I had to think quickly on my feet and my father's cure for insomnia by reading Dickens was the only thing that entered my mind.

"First off, most people are familiar with the story and second, when Ebenezer revisits the past, many truths about his life are uncovered."

In the faces before me, I saw glimpses of my father and pieces of his past. The photo I found triggered emotions of love and loss and a brilliant moment of lucidity for a man who was struggling to hold on to his sanity. *Why wouldn't I want that for them? Why wouldn't I want to give them the chance to uncover truths from their pasts?*

"Often jogging the memory can be difficult and...painful." I purposefully paused. There was no rustling of papers or cell phones clicking with texts. *They're listening...even when I'm unprepared they're listening.* I had the rapt attention of every adult in the room. *Huh. Maybe it's not a hobby. Maybe Ruth's right and I do have something they want.*

"Photos are helpful in kick-starting memories, but in the absence of that..." *In the absence of a key photo that has gone missing...oh.* The truth settled in my body. *Is that why Gorm took it? He saw his mom and a strange man behind her?*

"Um..." I shook my head. "Photos are memory jumpstarts, but when we don't have that to work with, I have a memory prompt that can really get the gray matter moving."

The seniors laughed. I looked at Vivian Jean. She was jovial and didn't seem to have a care in the world.

"Anything to get the gray matter moving, heck, I'm game for that!" Richard said.

"So am I," Jean said. "So am I."

At the conclusion of the class, I studied each of the faces of the students who passed my desk and handed in their in-class memory prompt. No one looked like anyone I had seen in my father's photo, but it was more than forty years old. Even Vivian, the sorrowful, blue-eyed beauty, had changed.

CHAPTER 19

"SHE'S STILL striking," I said to Ruth wrapping up a long explanation to her about my father, the photo, the college reunion in my class, oh, and that my father's unrequited love was Gorm's mom. *Wowza.*

"It's been a helluava day." I pinched the bridge of my nose. It didn't stop the throbbing between my eyes.

"Tell me more about this Vivian woman. I was a few years behind your father in school so I don't know many of his classmates. We're all around the same age, but I started college later."

"Well," I blew out a mouthful of air. After two hours of teaching, I was tired of hearing my own voice. "Like I said, she's still striking, *and* still turning heads, at least *Richard's*, but she wasn't..." I paused and brushed my finger across the edge of Ruth's desk. "She's not my mom."

Ruth's eyes softened. "Oh, Dani, I didn't think about that. Your dad may have loved this Vivian, but I *know* he was *in* love with your mother. He was courting her when I was in one of his classes. Cupid hit your father hard when he met your mom."

I reached up and started massaging my shoulders. The tension hadn't lessened, but thanks to Ruth my heart wasn't as heavy. "Thank you. You know, it wasn't hard to hear my dad talk about Vivian or *Jean*." I rolled my eyes. "In fact, it actually made me understand my father so *much* more. But..." I bit my bottom lip. "She was part of his past. Now..." I dropped my hands off my shoulder and shook my arms. I couldn't get the feeling of bad energy off me. "I don't know. Something's not right. Why is she suddenly in my class? My last name's listed on the course description in the catalog of classes, right?"

Ruth slowly nodded. "It is. You're thinking that if this Richard fella knew you were Joe Quinn's daughter, that..."

I put my finger on my nose. "Exactly. Quinn's not a super common name, not around here. Go to Ireland and it's another story, but Casper's no Ireland."

"Hmm." Ruth tapped her chin with her finger. "That is a bit odd."

"It's probably nothing but my overactive imagination." *And guilt. The things I did to her son are outlawed in some states.* I plunked down in the chair next to Ruth's desk. My briefcase was beside the chair and tipped over. The in-class writing assignment fell out.

"Great." I bent over to pick up the papers and they slipped out of my hand and fanned across the linoleum floor. "Really? Could this day *get* any worse?"

"Oh, don't say that, you'll jinx yourself." Ruth got out of her chair. I stayed in mine.

Jinx. Gorm. For a moment, I closed my eyes and imagined his lips against mine. The sweet taste of him and his arms wrapped around me was all I wanted. *I don't care who his mom is. Why should it matter? It's all part of their past, it doesn't have to be part of our future.*

"Dani?"

I opened my eyes. Ruth was on the floor, gathering sheets of loose-leaf paper.

"Oh, my gosh. Don't do that. It's my mess." I slid off my seat and joined Ruth on the floor.

She held the stack of papers close to her chest. Her grayish-green eyes favored green.

"What's wrong?"

"What did you have the students write about?"

"Um." My mind went blank. *Is this how dementia starts?* I pressed against the sides of my head and put my brain in an imaginary vice. *It was just an hour ago.* "Oh, yeah. Duh. Now I remember."

The expression on Ruth's face didn't change. It remained one of concern.

"I had each of the students close their eyes and mentally walk back through places from their past beginning with their childhood home."

Ruth listened as intently as the class had.

"While their eyes were closed, I asked questions like, what did your first home look like? What did it smell like? What did it feel like? What did it sound like? You know, I went through each of the five senses to tap into their sixth sense of intuition to pull those memories forward. Sometimes just the facts aren't enough. You need the emotion."

Ruth leaned toward me. "So that's all you discussed?"

I shrugged. "Yeah, well, I did have them open their eyes and write down their recollections. Why? Was I not supposed to do that? Did I break some rule?"

Great. What did I do wrong now? The familiar surge of adrenaline kicked in. "I just wanted to get a sampling of their writing to assess their skill level, that's all."

Ruth waved her hand to stop me. "Dani, you're not in trouble. You didn't do anything wrong." She handed me the stack of student papers. "But someone else did."

I held the papers out in front of me. The top sheet had three-holes punched along the margins, just like the other pages, but instead of the college-ruled paper covered with writing, it contained one sentence.

"Stop digging around where you don't belong."

CHAPTER 20

I THUMPED the palm of my hand against the double oak door. *If he's not home, I swear.* I rapped my knuckles hard against the front door. The door barely opened and Gorm's annoyingly sexy, recently shaved head was scarcely visible, when I launched into him.

"I need the photo back."

He stepped onto the front porch in a pair of blue jeans, gray thermal and a tantalizing cloud of cologne. "What?"

"The photo." I crossed my hands over my silk blouse. "From my Dad's desk. I need it back."

Gorm's face remained neutral. "I didn't take any photo."

"Really? You didn't take the photo with your mom in it?"

"No." The muscles in his face tightened.

Yeah. That's what I thought. "Well, James saw you take something."

Shock removed any tension in his face and replaced it with disbelief. It was the same look I had seen on Chase's face when I discovered his texts to Tanya. *That snake.*

My arms instinctively moved from across my chest to my

stomach. I literally felt sucker punched. "Oh my God. I actually started to trust you. I actually believed you."

"Dani, I didn't take the photo."

I pointed my finger at him. "You're lying to me."

He grabbed my finger. "No, I'm not."

I tried to pull away, but he dropped my finger and seized my wrist. He pulled me toward him. "I *did not* take that photo. I wouldn't do that to you. I love..."

What did he just say? I was inches away from him. *Did he say love?* His blue eyes were piercing and for a moment I knew the truth of his heart. For a moment I felt at peace.

"Dani, I didn't take the photo."

"I don't believe you." My chest started to shake and my eyes welled with tears. *Damn it. Damn it. Damn it. Not again.*

Gorm pulled me into him and wrapped his arms tightly around me. "Dani, I promise you, I did not take that photo."

I softly cried into his shirt. "But it's gone and James saw you take something and your face just now..."

If it was at all possible, Gorm held me closer. "I did see the picture and I was shocked that my mom and *your* dad were in it. But, I didn't take it. As God is my witness, I did *not* take it. I would never betray your trust like that."

I rolled my head to one side and leaned against his chest. *Why does he have to smell good?* "But James has a picture of you with the photo."

"Huh?"

I looked up at him. Streaks of black mascara marked his shirt. "James took a picture of you with his spy thing and you're holding the picture." I searched his eyes again.

Gorm's voice peaked. "I looked at it, but I didn't take it."

"Then what did you put in the back of your shorts?"

Gorm suddenly released me. "I'm sorry. I made a promise

and I don't break my promises."

"You made a promise?" I hit his chest with my hand. "To who? I thought we..." *What about those feelings of love?*

"Dani, it's not what you think."

I raised my hands up. "What am I supposed to think when you're not telling me anything other than you made a *promise* and you don't break promises? That's bullshit." *Why would he do this? Why would he say one thing and then pull away?*

"When the time is right and I can tell you, I will."

"Oh, do you *promise* you will?" My voice was snide and angry.

"Yes, I promise." His voice remained cool and collected.

"Whatever. You're promises aren't worth dick." Suddenly Richard's face surfaced in my mind. "I need to see if he's in the photo." I unconsciously voiced my subconscious thought.

"Who? What are you talking about?"

"What do you care? You stole something from my father's library, but promise you'll tell me when you can." I took a step away from him. "Well, I *promise* you, I'll be reporting your little crime to the community board as soon as I..." *Figure out who the hell to call and what to report.*

"Dani, what man do you need to see in the photo? The man standing by my mom?"

"No," I said with an annoyed tone to my voice. "I already *know* who he is." *And there's no Andrew's listed on my class roster.*

Gorm's face got ashen. He reached for the front door but it had swung open into the house. He steadied himself against the doorframe. He knelt over.

"Are you okay?" I was immediately beside him.

Gorm shook his head and spoke toward the deck floor. "Who is he? That man with my mom."

"Uh, all I know is what my dad told me."

Gorm looked up and grabbed my arm. He shook me hard. "What? What did he say?"

"You're scaring me." I pulled myself away and rubbed my arm, putting distance between us.

Gorm wiped his face with his hand. "Oh, my God. What have I done?" He reached for me. I backed away. "Dani, I'm sorry. You don't understand."

"You're right." I started to walk away. "I don't." *I don't understand you or how I could have fallen for you.*

"Please, don't leave."

His blue eyes had a haunted, hurt look and for a moment I saw his resemblance to his mother.

My voice softened. "His name is Andrew. I don't know his last name. I didn't ask. He was my father's best friend and he was in love with your mom." *So was my dad, but she didn't choose him. Seems to be a Quinn curse.*

I could see the pain on his face before he looked away and tried to hide it from me.

I spoke toward him. "My dad said your mom was in love with Andrew." I took a deep breath. "But he left. My Dad never knew why, only that it broke your mom's heart."

Gorm turned back toward me. His eyes were a mixture of confusion and sadness. He took a deep breath. "Thank you." He was still clearly shaken. "Uh...what man were you looking for?"

I shrugged. "Oh, I don't know I was trying to figure out if one of my students was in the photo."

Gorm let go of his grip on the house and walked toward me. "Why?"

"One of my students left an anonymous note warning to me to *stop digging around.*"

"What!" His melancholy suddenly turned to panic.

I held up my hand. "It's okay. It's nothing. It's probably some joke because they didn't want to do the memory exercise."

Gorm shook his head. "No, that doesn't sound like a joke."

"That's what Ruth said."

"Good. So you showed it to her."

"She found it."

Gorm brushed the stubble on his chin. "You think this has anything to do with the bones and that XYZ fraternity?"

I flew my hands up in front of me. "Who the hell knows? There's so much shit flying around, I'm beginning to feel like my dad and that I'm losing my mind."

Gorm laughed and my body embraced the sound. I smiled.

"Listen," I said. "I'm sorry. I didn't mean to come over here with guns a blazing. But the photo's gone and I *really* need to look at it and James saw you take something from my dad's library..."

"Dani, I did take something." He looked me straight in the eyes. "But it was given to me."

What? I quickly cataloged yesterday in my mind. *The last person Gorm was with was my brother.* "And you can't tell me what it was or who gave it to you?"

"That's right. I made a promise."

My brother wouldn't have kept anything else from me. He told me about dad's dementia. What else is there to tell? Gorm's lying.

"Are you okay?" he asked.

I felt sick to my stomach. *I don't know who to believe anymore.* I nodded.

"Hey, why don't you come in and let me fix you lunch?"

"No, thanks."

"Come on," he said. "I think I know how we can flush this guy out."

"Rain check?" I faintly smiled.

"Of course. You sure you're okay?"

My heart ached. I wanted to recklessly run into his arms and not look back. Instead, I studied his every feature. His strong jawline, Roman nose and those blue eyes that were impossible not to fall into.

"Dani?"

I faintly smiled. "Goodbye, Gorm."

CHAPTER 21

"JERK."

I tapped my foot on the floorboard of my Suburban and waited for the red traffic light to turn green. A week had passed since I had last spoken to or seen Gorm. *Thinking about him, however, was another story.*

"If he thinks I'm that naïve to believe my brother would lie to me..."

It had also been an uneventful week of instruction. No threats. No secret identities suddenly made known. No big deals. The veiled message on the paper was already a non-issue. It was probably as I suspected and someone who didn't want to dig up their past and complete the writing assignment.

"Does he really think I'm *that* stupid?" Still, I couldn't seem to let go of my last meeting with Gorm.

It was Saturday morning and the roads were free from traffic.

"Momma, who are you talking to?"

I glanced at James from my rearview mirror. His plastic shark pool toy and he were strapped into his car seat.

"Oh, baby, Momma was just talking to herself."

"More like ranting." Josie spoke from behind the cover of her teen vampire novel.

"I'm not ranting." I tilted the rearview mirror to see her better. "Josie, I'm not ranting."

She rolled her eyes. "Mom, whatever Gorm did made you *super* mad."

"He *stole* something from Grandpa." James leaned over in his car seat to spread the word to his sister.

The light turned green. I slowly accelerated through the intersection. "Gorm didn't *steal* anything." I still didn't know why I was giving him an alibi with my children. "And I'm not mad at him." *I'm hurt.*

Josie buried her head back in her book. I drove to the swimming pool and read every billboard in an attempt to redirect my attention. It didn't work. I was hoping the pool would.

I sat on the edge of the toddler pool in a white linen cover up. It was sheer, beautiful and showed hints of my bikini underneath. *Why the hell couldn't Gorm have seen me in this and not the Speedo?*

My feet swung below me in lukewarm pee water. I'm sure I had the handful of kids wading around in the pool to thank. James splashed and dunked his metallic painted shark in and out of the two-foot high water. The sun bounced a kaleidoscope of colors off the shark's dorsal fin.

"I'm going on the high dive."

Josie stood before me in her lemon-colored two-piece bathing suit. Her long limbs, undeveloped chest and taunt stomach were adorable in her bikini. With her long, dark hair, big eyes and thin frame, she reminded me of Popeye's girlfriend, Olive Oil.

"Please be careful."

"I will. I will."

"Okay, I'll be right here." I patted the warm concrete surrounding the pool with my hand.

Josie held up her thumb. "Got it."

I watched her walk to the adult pool...the same pool where I had shown off and swum the butterfly for Gorm. *Stupid. Stupid. Stupid. Why was I trying to impress him anyway? Stupid jerk.*

My cell phone was beside me and beeped with a text. It was from Ruth. *It's Saturday. What could she be texting?* I covered the screen to deflect the sun's glare.

"Did you see the paper this morning?"

James shrieked. I whipped my head toward his voice. His shark was being plowed down by another little boy's boat. They giggled and threw the shark in the air. I looked at my cell phone, hit the "reply" button and typed "No."

Seconds later my phone beeped again. "Where are you?"

"At the pool with kids." I hit "send" and then snapped my fingers. *Dang it. She's going to ask which pool.* I was typing 'Paradise Valley' when a call came through and bumped me off the text screen.

"This is Dani."

"Hi."

His voice was low, husky and scratchy. It was the sound of a seasoned smoker. It was the sound of Chase.

My stomach jumped, but it wasn't from butterflies taking flight. It was from butterflies dropping to their death.

"Well," he said. "I was kind of counting on this going to voicemail, but I'm glad that it didn't. It would have been hard to say on a message."

I listened while I watched James in the kiddie pool. He was happy, frolicking and in five-year-old heaven.

"Are you there?"

I nodded into the phone.

"Dani, hello? Anyone there."

"Uh, yeah, I'm here."

"How's city life?"

I rolled my eyes. Casper wasn't a city, but it wasn't the rural farm area I had left either. "It's great, how are you?" *I can talk pleasantries, too.*

"Oh, I'm hanging in there. It sure is quiet in the house without you all here."

Anger stirred in my stomach. *I bet it is. That's what happens when...*I stopped my thoughts midway. *Don't. I'm doing so well. Don't go backwards. He's not worth it.*

"So what are you calling about Chase?"

I spotted Josie on the high dive and waved to her. I held my thumb up. She grinned and then proceeded to walk off the diving board and straight into the pool. I started to laugh and held the phone away from my mouth. Josie wasn't a diver or even a cannon baller, nope, my girl liked to walk the plank.

"So..." Chase's voice resonated in my ear. "I saw a ring like your Dad's in the newspaper and that whole article about the bones they found at the college. I was wondering if you knew anything else."

My hand started shaking. "What article? What do you mean?" *This must be what Ruth was texting about. What now?*

"Oh, ho, ho. Looks like I got the scoop on the famous writer."

"I'm not famous and you know it." *When did Chase start reading the statewide paper? The local paper's death and divorce announcements were about all that held his interest. And that was merely to hit up for garage or estate sales. Damn coyote.* "So you haven't read the morning paper. Did you perhaps have a late Friday night?"

"Well, thanks for the heads up about the article. I'll have to go check that out." I scanned the snack shack in the distance.

There didn't appear to be a newspaper stand. I held the phone up to my ear and realized there had been a noticeable pause. I smiled "Yeah, you do that. Go grab a paper and read it. Let me know if you have any other information about that, okay."

His interest was just odd. "Sure. Will do, Chase."

I was about to hang up when James splashed up beside me. *He hasn't even asked about our son.* "Um, would you like to talk to..."

"Oh, hey," Chase cut me off. "I better get back to chasing cows."

"Chase." I stood up and quickly took a step away from the pool so James wouldn't hear me. "James would love to talk to you."

"Can't do that."

"What do you mean?"

"Listen, you decided to move my son hundreds of miles away. I get to decide how I handle it. And I'm not ready to talk to him."

"But he's only five."

"You probably should have thought about that before you took off to go live the big city life."

The distant and all-too-familiar sound of the call disconnecting rang loudly in my ear. I held the phone away from me and stared. My eyes stung with tears. *How does he still do that to me?*

"You okay?" Ruth stood on the other side of the fence to the toddler pool.

"You found us."

"I did. Spotted your big red tank in the parking lot. Now stop diverting the question, are you okay?"

"Ah, I let him do it again."

"Who? Who did what?"

I mouthed Chase's name to Ruth so James wouldn't hear. "I let him get to me again. I took the bait." My hand formed into a fist and I punched the air. "I was doing so well, too."

"Oh, well, ex's are skilled at pushing our buttons. The key is to stop having buttons to push."

"Sure." I opened my clenched fist like I was magician releasing a dove. "And that's so easy to do."

Ruth chuckled and tilted her head toward the gate. "Okay if I come in?"

"Absolutely. You might get splattered with water..."

"Ah, heck," Ruth waved the air. "That's nothing. Despite what my ex may say, water won't make me melt."

I smiled. *It's got to be a gift. Ruth's timing, her ability to say the right things, make me laugh when I want to cry. What would I do without her?*

Ruth walked in with a newspaper tucked under her arm.

"Do I *even* want to know?"

She extended the folded paper toward me. A table and chairs were positioned off in the distance behind her.

"Just a minute." I walked over and dragged the table closer to the pool.

"James." My son stopped flapping his arms in the water. "I'm going to be right here." I pointed toward a white plastic chair that Ruth hauled over.

"Okay. Hi, Miss Ruth!" He waved at my one and only friend in Casper.

"Hey, there James! You look great in the water."

He beamed. "I know."

We both laughed.

"Oh, if only I had that amount of confidence." I put a towel on the chair and sat.

Ruth pushed the front page toward me.

Human Remains Uncovered at Cowboy U

I put my hand over my mouth and stared at the headline. *Oh no.* I glanced at the byline and felt my chest deflate with air. *He didn't.*

By Chris Gorham, Times Staff Writer

"He actually did a nice job with the piece," Ruth said.

I picked up the paper and started to read.

Dishing out dirt is nothing new to Bob Dorsey.

"Oh my God! He used Bob." I gripped the paper in my hand. I'm sure fumes were probably visible from my head.

Ruth waved me down. "It's okay. Bob gave him permission."

"Really? What about whistle blowers and losing his job?"

Ruth raised her shoulders. "Bob said and I'm quoting him directly, 'my boss is a real dick. If I get fired, it'll be a blessing.'"

"Huh."

Ruth nudged her head toward the paper. "Keep reading."

Dishing out dirt is nothing new to Bob Dorsey. The maintenance worker at Cowboy State University was doing just that when the blade on the backhoe he operated stopped working.

"I struck something hard," he said with a laugh. "Usually Bertha (the name he christened his backhoe) can get through anything. But on that day, well, she was as stubborn as a mule."

Dorsey expected to find a water pipe or perhaps a boulder. What he found shocked the thirty-two-year-old California native.

"I couldn't believe it," he said. "I looked into the hole and I saw a skull staring back at me. It freaked me out."

Though startled, Dorsey had the presence of mind to contact the foreman with Birdseye Construction. Birdseye Construction was awarded the University's building contract with the written caveat that the Denver-based firm employed the college's classified staff.

"It's a political thing, really," Dorsey said. "Since the college isn't employing us year-round it drops our status to part-time employees so we aren't eligible for healthcare benefits."

Dorsey notified Birdseye Construction foreman Bill Hull of the findings, who according to Dorsey didn't seem surprised.

"That's the thing that initially stuck out to me. This guy didn't even bat an eye when I pulled out the skull and walked it over to him. It's almost like he was expecting it," Dorsey said.

I tilted down the newspaper. "Do you think the construction company knew about this before they dug?"

Ruth turned the palms of her hands up. "It's hard to know. It sure sounds like this Hull character knew something."

"Huh." I resumed reading.

According to Dorsey, Cowboy University officials contacted a university anthropologist and geologist to inspect the remains.

"They both confirmed that they're human bones and not the fossil remains of a dinosaur," Dorsey said, who was present during the evaluations.

"It was pretty wild," Dorsey said.

The backhoe operator expected the local authorities to be contacted next.

"Wouldn't you think that the police would be called? Instead, they bagged up the bones along with an old concrete bag that was beside the remains and stuffed it in a kitchen cabinet in a trailer," Dorsey said.

According to city building permits, the University's last expansion project began in the spring of 1964. Hawkeye Construction, the parent company of Birdseye, was the construction company on record.

I stared at the date. *1964.* "April would be considered spring, right?"

Ruth nodded. "Why?"

"The photo I found, it was date stamped April 1964 the same time the University was under construction." *Maybe Gorm was right about flushing someone out. No. He couldn't be right.* I snapped the paper and creased it along the fold and continued reading.

Without the support of the University, Dorsey contacted the Times and offered complete access to the bones. Among the remains, a ring was found.

"I thought it was just some ordinary ring, but if you look closer into the center of the stone, there's the Greek letters X, Y, Z. A friend of mine told me it means Xi Upsilon Zeta, but the 'Y' can be used as either a 'Y' or a 'U' in the Greek alphabet. Apparently it was a fraternity ring for an academic underground group who called themselves, 'The XYZ Affair' after the historical event with the French," Dorsey said.

The University was contacted for this story, but refused to comment. To date, the human bones and their identity remain in a decrepit concrete bag tucked in a portable trailer's kitchen cabinet.

"Ah," I looked over the paper at Ruth. "Bob called me his friend and he remembered all my ramblings."

Ruth smiled. "I think Gorm helped fill in some of the quotes. He did a real nice job with this story."

I shooed away her remark and hid behind the paper. Two

photos accompanied the centerpiece story, one of the ring and one of Bob beside the bag of bones.

"How'd Gorm get the ring?" *Did that little bastard take it that night?*

"The story says Bob gave the Times full access. I figure when they took pictures of the bones, Bob showed him the ring too."

I grimaced. "Yeah, but...Gorm *knew* about the ring. Maybe he had it with him?"

"Why would Gorm have the ring?"

I shrugged. "I don't know."

Ruth smiled. "I think you're beginning to see conspiracy everywhere you turn. I really think Bob just opened the bag and let the photographer snap away. The ring was definitely cleaned up, but that makes sense. They want to gather as much information from the public as they can."

"What do you mean?"

Ruth tilted her head. "Read the box by the pictures."

A small text box was off to the side, along the margin of the paper.

The Times is offering a reward for any information pertaining to this story.

And there it is. That's why Chase called. *Sonuvabitch. He wants the cash.*

"Wow." I set down the newspaper. Bob stared up at me from the page. "Did he get fired?"

"Not yet."

Ruth leaned toward me and patted my hand. "Dani, I know the last time you spoke to Gorm things didn't go so well."

I rolled my eyes. "He lied to me. He took something from my father's library and lied to me about who gave it to him. *If* someone even gave him anything. I still haven't found the picture."

Ruth sat back in her chair. "There are always two sides to every story."

I threw my hands in the air. "Really? The photo's still missing and Gorm's had an entire week to clear up any misgivings. He's remained on his side of the proverbial fence and I've stayed on mine." *I've waited for him to call, but he hasn't.*

"Do you really believe that?"

"What?"

"That he's distanced himself from you."

I grabbed my cell phone and shook it. "In a week's time there haven't been any missed calls or voicemail messages from him." *Jerk.* I shrugged. "It doesn't matter. Guilt will do that to a person."

"Oh, Dani, you really care about him."

I put down my cell phone. "Cared. Past tense. I *cared* about him, but not anymore."

"That's a shame because after reading his story I couldn't help but think that Gorm was trying to divert the attention off you. From what you told me, that note you got in class really seemed to unnerve him."

I crossed my arms over my chest. "Oh, what do I know? I doubt it had any bearing on this. Gorm just found a way he could write the story and dump it on Bob."

"Dani, that's not fair. Bob agreed to this story, and Gorm's putting himself out there too."

"How do you figure that? This is an above the fold front-page story. Any reporter would *die* for this piece."

"Um, I'm not so sure."

"Okay, I'll bite. Why wouldn't a reporter want this story?"

"For the same reason, I was resistant to come forward with what I knew. Like any small town, our little community is governed by a handful of wealthy people. Ticking off the wrong folks is never a good or wise professional move."

I uncrossed my arms and laid my hands in front of me on the table. My ring finger was bare and now probably its permanent state.

Ruth picked up the newspaper and folded it back together. "The writer of this story," she gently tapped his byline, "man, he took a big risk and put the bullseye on himself. Gorm did this for you."

"Damn it. Why can't you just be a cute, bubble-headed friend that holds my hair back when I puke and drive me home when I'm drunk?"

Ruth threw her head back and started laughing. "If that's what you need."

"No. I need someone that's willing to tell me the truth even when I don't want to hear it. Even when I'm not sure I fully believe it."

Ruth smiled. "I know."

I looked over and saw Josie climb the high dive ladder.

"Hey, would you mind watching James for a minute?"

"Sure."

I pulled off my cover up and walked in my tangerine-colored bikini toward the deep end. My hips swayed and I thought of Gorm. *I love your curves and hourglass figure.*

I stood behind Josie on the ladder. She was next in line.

"Hey, little girl."

She held onto the sides of the ladder and turned her head. "Oh my gosh! Are you going to dive?"

I moved my head up and down.

A wide smile crossed her face. "Yeah! You *never* do that."

"I know. But this very wise girl once told me I have to try new things."

She flipped her wet hair back. "Well, you know, I am smart-a-cull."

Josie was always creating new words. This was her latest. I grinned. "You're smart-a-cull and lovable."

She strode with confidence to the edge of the board and walked right off it. It never ceased to make me laugh.

I waited until Josie had swum to the side of the pool before I made my way to the final step on the ladder. *I hate heights.* I looked out at the body of water. *I also hate liars.* My steps suddenly had purpose. *But I really hate not knowing the truth. Or how he really feels. Why hasn't he called?* I reached the end of the diving board and looked down. The water's surface was surprisingly smooth.

I saw my daughter smiling and my son waving. Yet something inside me felt incomplete. *I miss him. Damn it I barely know him and I miss him.* I stared at the bottom of the pool and hoped there was enough water to wash him out of me.

CHAPTER 22

"Daniella, will you please join your mother and me in the library."

I looked at Josie and James who were eating a bowl of ice cream at the breakfast bar. I stuck out my tongue. "I'm being summoned."

They giggled.

"Josie, will you keep an eye on James for me?"

"Sure will."

I grabbed my cup of coffee off the counter and headed toward my parents' beckoned call. *I've got to reschedule an appointment with the realtor.*

"Oh, there she is!" My father bounded out of his executive chair and walked around his desk to greet me.

I looked at my mom and then back at my dad. They were both giddy. *Oh gross. Did they have sex while we were at the pool?*

"Sit down, sit down." My father pulled forward one of his side chairs. It was across from my mom.

I sat down and placed my coffee on a coaster on his desk.

My dad took his seat and looked at me. "Daniella, we read Chris' story in the paper today."

Oh crap. Here it comes.

"What a fine young man to tackle such a controversial, alleged subject." The professor surfaced and I could hear the subtle university politics beneath his words.

"There's nothing alleged about it. I saw the bones." The words slipped out of my mouth as sudden as the thought. *Damn that's gonna bring a shit storm.*

My father tilted his head. "You saw the bones?"

"Yes, I did." I pulled my hair back and grabbed Josie's ponytail holder off my wrist with my teeth. I wrapped the soft covered rubber band around my hair and pulled until it hurt. I was willing to do anything to avoid looking at my dad, who intently stared at me.

"I was not aware of that fact." My father pulled on the sleeve of his shirt. It tightened and aligned perfectly along his arm. "Daniella, why do you continue to focus on something so inconsequential instead of your career?"

Ah, the return of the professor. Didn't think the kinder, softer, dad would last long. "Well at least I'm not focusing on another man, right, Dad?"

"Daniella, buried bones are simply another distraction from your career. I do not understand how you could be so reckless, especially considering your financial situation."

Asshole. "My financial situation is solid. I have no debt, an older, but," I raised my finger in the air for emphasis, "paid for Suburban, enough in savings to put down on a house. Oh, and did I mention, no debt? My financial situation is solid. Our relationship on the other hand..." I turned my head in disgust only to whip it around a second later and stare down my father. "Make up your mind," I blurted out. "Either be a decent human being to me or an ass, but you can't be both."

"Joseph." My mom's voice cut through the tension in the library. "This is *not* why we asked to speak to Daniella."

My father cleared his throat. "I wasn't aware that you had been part of this ruse to unearth bones at the college, but since you did, I want no part of whatever else you discover. Professionally, it is not in my best interest to be involved."

Of course not. "It wasn't like I was trying to get you involved or keep this big secret," I said in my defense. "I promised my friend that I wouldn't tell anyone about the bones and I didn't. I never involved you nor did I intend to."

My father's voice softened, "Well, a promise is a promise. I understand that." His reasoning hit me square in the stomach.

A promise is a promise.

"That's actually what we wanted to talk to you about," he said.

Great. The hits keep coming. I reached for my coffee and took a sip. The sweet taste of caramel and the delicate hint of mocha blended together and awakened my mouth.

"Daniella, in light of recent medical issues." My father navigated around the topic of his possible dementia with the skill of a politician sidestepping an issue. "Your mother and I had living wills drawn up and among the necessary paperwork was a medical DNR."

DNR. I blanked. "What's that again?"

His eyes softened and so did his voice.

"Daniella, in the event, I should become incapacitated and I am unable to breathe or function on my own, I have a 'Do Not Resuscitate' order that would need to be given to the hospital."

I placed my coffee back on the coaster and wagged my finger. "Oh, no. I can't. I won't." A heaviness weighed on my chest. "I'm not going to be the one to pull the plug on you. No way. I'm not living with that."

My mom reached over and grabbed my hand. "Well, hopefully I'll be around to do that."

"But if you're not?" My voice was brittle with emotion. "Then what?"

"Initially we were hoping that either you or Finnegan would act as our intermediaries with the hospital or medics, whatever the case may be," she said.

I vehemently shook my head. "I'm sorry. I can't do it."

My mom squeezed my hand. I held onto it for dear life. "I'm sorry, but I can't."

My father leaned forward in his chair. "Your brother knew that. He said you wouldn't be able to do it. So he had the smart sense to ask Chris if he'd be willing to serve in that capacity."

"Gorm?" *Oh no*. "When did he do this? When did Finn talk to him?"

"Oh, when Finnegan was here during Memorial Day week," my mom said. "He spoke to Chris and Chris assured him, actually, *promised* your brother that he would step up on your behalf."

My heart was in my throat. "Did Finn give Gorm the DNR?"

My father nodded. "He did. The night before Finnegan flew home he spoke to Chris – right here in my library. He gave Chris the DNR *that* night."

"Oh my God."

My father scurried out of his chair and came around to where I sat. "Daniella, what's wrong?"

I couldn't speak. I looked at him. *Please. Please be kind to me.* Tears ran down my face.

He reached up and wiped one away. "What is it sweetheart?"

"You were worried that Gorm might break my heart." I swallowed the knot in my throat.

My father nodded.

I let go of my mom's hand and put my hand on my chest. "He didn't," I said and lowered my head. I began to weep. "I broke his."

CHAPTER 23

I'VE SCREWED up *again. I'm twice divorced and now this.* I lowered my head only to feel the tears that had collected beneath my eyes now run down my face. I sat with my back against the bed in the guest bedroom with my legs stretched out in front of me. Josie and James were watching a movie. I couldn't concentrate on anything, but the shambles of my life.

Sometimes I don't even think that it's me. When I think about being divorced twice I think in terms like it happened to someone else. Because this is not how my life was supposed to go.

I cried and crawled to the bay window. I knelt in front of it. Three window panels dissected the horizon. I looked out the right pane of glass and into the setting sun. I didn't know whom I was praying to. I just hoped someone was listening.

"What do you want from me? What is this all about? What's the purpose of this *masterful plan* you have laid out for me?" I pinched my nose together and wiped my snotty hand on my jeans.

A low, sorrowful murmur began in my throat and slowly

seeped out of my mouth. I sounded like a wounded animal. This only made me cry harder. I placed my hands on my thighs to stop the trembling.

"Please. Just tell me what you want from me because I can't have another failed anything. Not now. Not ever. I'm sorry for screwing up my life, but it's dominoed its way down to my children. They like him. All my children like Gorm." I couldn't breathe. I sobbed and felt tears land on my hands.

Sentences were stuck in my throat. Sentences like, "I need your help." "Show me the truth." "Do you hear me?" and then the final one that just couldn't find its way to be verbalized, "Does he really love me?"

I sniffled, but snot kept running out of my nose and into my mouth. "I can't keep doing this? I can't keep wondering, is this the one? Will he stay now? Will he love me after he's had me?"

I bent over my knees and slammed the hardwood floor with the palm of my hand. The smack stung but made me feel alive. "Why do I even need someone? Why does this matter? It shouldn't matter."

But it did. My heart was sunk and synced with Gorm. I couldn't help it. He had done the one thing I had promised myself I would never allow to have happen again: He had fallen for me the way I had for him.

"Now what?" I swallowed and tried to push down the hurt that was lodged in my throat. I looked up. The sun had taken its final bow. It broke through the clouds and shone down on me. The top of my head felt warm.

"What do I do now? Now that I..." I couldn't even say the word.

"Love him?"

My mother's voice came from behind me.

I nodded, but I didn't turn around.

"Oh, Dani." She knelt down beside me and placed her hand on my back. "It's okay to want to be loved and to love someone."

I shook my head. "No. Not with my track record. Not after just a few days. I hardly know him...It's a nightmare."

She rubbed my back. "Love is never a nightmare."

I turned and looked at her. "Mom, it's never been anything, *but* a nightmare."

"Dani, that's just not true. I remember how happy you were on your wedding days to Mike and to Chase. You loved those men and they loved you."

My body shook. "They just didn't *stay* in love with me."

"And shame on them, but that's not your shame to bear."

"Mom." I wiped my nose on the sleeve on my shirt. "I'm the common denominator."

"You weren't Chase's first wife and you probably won't be his last."

I slightly smiled.

"And you and Mike outgrew each other. You were so young when you married him."

My breathing slowed down and so did my crying. I rubbed my eyes and then looked at her. "You were young when you got married. Did you ever outgrow Dad?"

Her eyes welled. "No. Never. If anything, I always worried he'd outgrow me. Your father is a brilliant man."

My heart understood her insecurity.

"Mom, I think I finally met a good guy. A really good guy and I screwed up." I kept my focus locked onto her face. Her eyes were identical in color with her favored grandchild, Michael.

She placed her hand on top of mine. "What happened?"

I stared into her hazel eyes. "There was this photo. It's a long story, but I accidentally found it, then it disappeared and I accused Gorm of taking it."

"Why would you do that?" My mom was genuinely so good. She couldn't image being cruel to anyone.

"I'm not like you. I'm mean and guarded."

She squeezed my hand. "Daniella Maureen, I don't believe that for a minute. Now, why would you think Gorm would take this picture?"

"Because his mom was in it."

She closed her eyes. "Is his mom...Vivian?"

"Yes. But...how'd you know? Does dad know?"

She opened her eyes, lifted her head and looked at the ceiling. "Your father doesn't know. But, dear, Lord what have I done?"

"Mom, what are you talking about?"

She grabbed my hand and held it against her heart. "Daniella, *I* took that picture."

"What?"

"I have lived with the ghost of that woman for more than forty years. When I saw Vivian's beautiful young smiling face on your father's desk, well, I had enough."

"I don't understand."

"There's so much history with that picture." She exhaled a slow, steady breath. "I shot the photo."

"What?" My voice was alarmingly high and panicked. "What do you mean you *shot* the photo? Couldn't you have just thrown it away or burnt it?"

She laughed. "No sweetheart, I originally *shot* the photo. I was hired by the University's country club to be their banquet photographer. That's the night I met your father."

"*Ohhh.*" It made sense. My mom enjoyed photography, which is why we had so many photo albums. What I didn't know was that she had once made a career of it. I knew my grandfather had, but I didn't know she had followed in her father's footsteps. Still there was something that didn't make sense.

"How did you know Vivian was Gorm's mom?"

She softly smiled. "He has her eyes."

I started crying. "I know." I looked at my mom. "But they aren't as sad as his mom's."

"No, but they are just as haunted."

I wiped my eyes on the sleeve of my shirt. "They are, aren't they?"

My mom nodded. "It's the first thing I noticed when I snapped that dinner photo in the sixties. Vivian's face captured the lens, but so did her eyes. They were so beautifully sad and so tragically haunted."

I listened.

"Last summer when Chris moved into the neighborhood your father and I brought him a welcoming plant." She rolled her eyes. "You know your father and his idea of a housewarming gift."

We both chuckled.

"I had my camera gear in the car and your father *insisted* I snap his photo with the local sports writer and our new neighbor. You dad was just enamored with Chris's talent for writing."

"That's when you thought he was Vivian's son?"

"No, it wasn't that clear cut. I was adjusting the lens to focus on your father and Chris when these eyes looked back at me. I pulled away from the camera and looked at this young man. I remember thinking there was no way he could be related to Vivian. But I had never seen such beautiful blue eyes that were as haunted as hers until I took Chris' photo."

"Did you ask him if he was Vivian's son?"

"Oh, heaven's no." She released my hand and rested her hands in her lap. "But I did inquire into his family background." She started to laugh.

"What'd he say?" I found myself smiling.

"The truth. That his mother was Jean Gorham."

"Vivian Jean."

She nodded. "Until you just said that his mom was in that photo, I hadn't remembered her initials."

"How'd you even know them?"

"Oh, back in the day it was quite the fashion statement to have a purse or anything monogrammed with your initials. Vivian's purse is on the table in the picture. It's off to the side, but I remember the rich, black velvet material and the white embroidery. Her initials are as clear to me today as they were some forty years ago: V. J. W."

"Vivian Jean Wilson," I said.

"That's right. Daniella, how did you know? Did Chris tell you?"

"No, he's never spoken about his parents, but I've never asked either."

Her face looked puzzled.

"Vivian or *Jean* as she prefers to be called is one of the students in my class."

My mom gasped. "Oh, no."

"Mom," I wrapped my arm around her and held her tightly. "She's a lovely woman, but she's not you. Not by a long shot."

"Daniella." She kissed the top of my head. "Thank you, but... that must be awkward to have her in your class."

I chuckled. "Actually, it isn't. She's just one of the lovely seniors I get to talk very loudly to."

She elbowed me. "Hey, there, I'm in that senior class."

"Mom, you're in a class all your own. She can't hold a candle to you."

She tilted her head and smiled. "Oh, darling, thank you."

"I mean it. I wouldn't lie to you."

"I know."

"I'm so sorry about unearthing that picture. I never meant to hurt you. I didn't know who she was or what it was about."

My mom held me tightly against her. "Dani, how could you know? It's not your fault. I'm the one...Oh Lord, what a mess I've made."

I rested my head against her. "No, you didn't. I did that all by myself."

"With your dad's memories starting to fade," she spoke in my hair. "I didn't want him to think of Vivian or worse think that I was her. I've always known I wasn't his first choice. I saw the way he looked at her that night at the banquet and I hoped one day he'd look at me that way too."

She shook her head. "It's foolish, but I didn't want a visual reminder of the woman you're dad first loved. I got scared so I hid the photo. I just wanted her and the memory of her out of our lives."

"Do you still have it? The picture?"

She nodded. "Yes as much as I would have *loved* to destroy it, it still has fond memories for me as a photographer."

I smiled. "Do you remember who else was in that picture?"

"Oh, my memory's better than your father's, but that'd be tough. I remember Andrew."

"Vivian's date?"

"Oh, he was more than Vivian's date. I heard them talk about getting married."

I slapped my hand against my chest. "You're kidding?"

"Not at all. I was taking a photo of the table behind them and I heard bits and pieces of their conversation."

"Was Dad there?"

"No, he had gone somewhere. Maybe up to the podium? He was giving out an award that night. There was another man still at the table. I don't remember his name, but he was..." My mom cringed. "He was creepy. He had his back turned to Vivian and Andrew, but I could tell he was hanging onto their every word."

I grabbed her hand and squeezed it. "Now, Mom, I need for you to really remember something."

Her hazel eyes widened. "Okay."

"Did this man have on one of those rings? You know, like Dad's fraternity rings?"

She smiled. "No, this man was not a member of the XYZ Affair."

I nudged her in the side. "Well, look at you Miss Thing, talking about Dad's fraternity and the XYZ Affair."

She chuckled. "Dani, that's what the banquet was called, The XYZ Affair. It was in honor of the University's political science department. Only a handful of men there were also part of the academic fraternity. It was the event of the season."

"But the man that was eavesdropping on Vivian and Andrew, he wasn't a member of the fraternity?"

"No and he was barely hanging on as a student in the political science department. I remember the men at another table mocking him for even being there. Supposedly, he was on academic probation, but that didn't prevent him from being a loud mouth about his future career in construction."

My heart rate soared. "Mom, do you remember if he mentioned the name of the company where he was going to begin this big construction career?"

"Of course, it was Hawkeye Construction."

My heart was beating so loudly it echoed in my ears.

She continued, "Everyone recognized the construction company because it was on campus, but no one cared for this guy. It was actually, rather sad."

"Why did he even go to the banquet, this XYZ Affair, if no one liked him?"

"His date. Her father owned Hawkeye Construction Company. I suppose he wanted to look like a big shot. It was pretty pathetic. I felt sorry for him."

I rubbed my forehead. "But you don't remember his name?"

She made a clacking sound with her tongue. "I wish I could. Your father may?"

"But you don't want him to see the photo."

She exhaled. "Not really, but if it's important to you."

"I don't even know what's important anymore. Gorm wrote that story about the bones and the ring. Dad's upset about it, even though he won't admit it." I threw my hands up in the air. "The ironic thing is that whoever's bones they unburied was probably a member of Dad's XYZ fraternity. So this loudmouth guy probably doesn't even matter. I only asked because he was the only man at the table not wearing one of those rings. That's why he stood out to me."

My mom proudly smiled. "So you've got a bit of your mother's eye for detail."

"I guess I do," I said equally as proud.

For a moment neither of us spoke. Despite the fluctuating emotions I had for my dad, I knew how important he was to my mom.

"You know Dad loves *you*. He married *you*. Vivian was..." I looked over at her. "Mom, she's just not you. She's not full or life. There's still something sad about her."

Her face softened in the early evening light. "Daniella, you have such a good heart."

I looked into her eyes. "Then what do I do? What do I do now? Vivian is Gorm's mom, how is this *ever* going to work, knowing how you feel about her? I can't be with Gorm. It's not right. It's not fair to you."

My mom reached out and held my hand. "How I feel about

Vivian is not the issue. It's how you feel about Chris that is."

"No, I can't be with him. Could you imagine family barbeques? You, Dad, Vivian and her husband? *Awkward.*"

She laughed. "Let's take this one step at a time. And the first step now, sweet child is for you to stop being so nasty to that nice sports writer. He's a good man, a *very* good man."

I smiled. "I know he is."

She squeezed my hand. "So go to him. Apologize, tell him your mom's the thief, and beg for his forgiveness. And then," She kissed me on the forehead. "tell the man how you feel. Dani, don't wait. Life's too short. Tell Chris you love him."

CHAPTER 24

THE MICROWAVE in my parents' house was the only relic they hadn't updated. My father refused to part with the first microwave he bought in the early eighties. It had a turn style table that barely made a full rotation in a minute's time.

"Oh dear God." I opened the door to the brown-colored microwave that took up an entire corner of their kitchen. "Really Dad? It's time for an upgrade."

I placed my coffee cup in the center and wound the timer past the minute mark.

"Here goes nothing."

The window-paneled door glowed and the machine hummed. I rolled my neck and tried in vain to release the tension. *I need a massage.* The seconds were loudly ticking by on the ancient timer. *No, I need Gorm.* He still hadn't returned the message I left him last night.

"Okay," I bargained with myself, "if he still hasn't called by the time James wakes up from his nap or Mom and Dad return from the matinee with Josie, then I'll go over and knock on his door."

I watched the timer tick down. I wanted to hit *stop* before the archaic buzzer dinged. *James needs to nap. Me too.* Within seconds of the minute mark, I quietly opened the door and reached in for my coffee cup. The handle stung with heat. I instinctively recoiled. The cup fell from my hands. I jumped away as it shattered on the tile floor. Coffee began to seep into the tan-colored grout.

"Shit!" My voice echoed in the kitchen.

I covered my mouth with my burnt hand and held my breath. In the distance, I heard James begin to cry.

"Shit! Shit! Shit! Damn you old stupid machine!"

James' crying intensified.

"I'm coming, honey." I tiptoed out of the kitchen and poked my head down the hallway. I spoke through the slots in the banister and raised my voice so he could hear it upstairs. "Momma's coming, baby. I gotta clean this up first."

When I walked back into the kitchen, the coffee had seeped across more of the tile. The bottom of my flip-flops slid across the glassy surface and I fell smack down in the middle of broken glass. The palm of my hand burned with the pinprick pain from slivers of ceramic that covered the top layer of my already coffee-scorched skin. I shook my hand and chunks of glass flew across the room.

I wanted to scream, but I wanted five more minutes alone so I squelched the urge.

I reached for a dishtowel and carefully brushed my hands. With the tip of my flip-flop, I collected the larger pieces of glass and pushed the pile toward the oven.

I laid the towel on the floor and watched the surrounding puddle of dark liquid absorb into the cotton dishrag. *What a freaking mess.*

I stood still and listened for James. I heard the faint sound of him talking. I exhaled slowly and quietly.

Please, just a few more minutes. Then I'll get James and clean up this disaster.

I leaned against the dishwasher and gently slid down the door. I sat with my back propped against it and my legs outstretched. I folded my hands in my lap and closed my eyes.

I didn't hear him enter the kitchen nor did I see him. Rather I felt him. I opened my eyes and Gorm was crouched down in front of me.

"Hey." He placed his hand on my knee. The warmth was electric. "You okay?"

"You're here." My throat tightened. "I can't believe you're here." I blinked to make sure I hadn't hit my head when I slipped and that I wasn't hallucinating.

"The front door was unlocked. I hope it was okay that I..."

"You're here!" *There's still hope...*

He smiled. "Well, your mom left a pretty urgent note on my door for me to come see you."

"Ahh."

"I've been outta town."

"Ohhh." *So he wasn't avoiding me.*

Gorm nervously looked around. "Where's Izzy?"

I laughed. "It's okay. She's not lost."

The muscles in his face relaxed.

I smiled. "Izzy's at the pet groomers – courtesy of my mom."

"That's classic."

Crouched in front of me, we looked at each other.

"It was pretty great when I got back into Wyoming cell phone range and discovered I had a really sweet voicemail message from this hot teacher."

I smiled widely.

Gorm surveyed the kitchen floor. "Did you fall?"

"Slipped."

"Oh, Dani." Gorm extended his hand. "Come on, let's get you cleaned up."

I was still parked against the dishwasher. I reached for his hand and the contact sent a sharp pain through me. I snapped it back.

"Okay, okay." Gorm reached around to the side of his belt and unhooked a Leatherman pocketknife. He opened the multi-purpose tool to the needle nose pliers. Gorm switched from crouching to putting one knee down on the floor and the other one up. I knew from watching Finn play football, Gorm was "taking a knee" and it was sexy. The care he showed every time I needed him never ceased to surprise me.

"May I have your hand?" he asked.

At this point, I'd give you anything. I placed my hand palm up in his. His course hand dwarfed mine. The tanned rough texture and his large padded-like fingers reminded me of a baseball mitt.

"How do you type with those things? Your hands are huge."

"Carefully," he said without looking up. He leaned over me and gently pulled out a thin sliver of glass with his pliers. He held it up in the air.

"Got'cha."

I let out a sigh of relief. "I hate splinters of any kind...glass, wood." I shuddered. "Thank you." *You're my hero.*

Gorm held onto my hand and inspected it for more glass.

"Okay, other hand."

I exchanged hands at his command. His blue eyes locked their sapphire-colored rays onto my palm. I instantly felt warmer. I leaned toward him.

He looked up. A crooked grin curved his lips. "You're blocking my light."

I shrugged. "Whatta ya going to do 'bout it?" I braced myself against the dishwasher and wrapped my legs around his waist.

"Dani..." He looked at me.

I smiled and pulled him toward me.

"What about James?"

"I think he went back to sleep."

"You think?"

I tilted my head and listened. Nothing. I raised an eyebrow and grinned.

"Really? Right here in the kitchen?"

I started to pull away. "If you're not into it..."

"No. I'm not saying that." Gorm glanced at the oven and the covered pile of glass. He scooted me away from the broken remains. When I was safely out of reach from the glass and spilled coffee, he looked at me.

Kiss me. Kiss me already.

"I'm sorry," I said. "I should've believed you when you said you didn't take the photo. I..."

He put his finger to my lips. "Shh."

I smiled. *Where'd he learn that move? Oh, yeah. That's my move.*

"Um," he looked around. "Won't your parents be coming home soon?"

I shrugged. "Maybe..."

His eyes danced with excitement. Gorm grabbed me by the waist and I slid on the tile beneath him. He leaned down and whispered in my ear. "Dani, I will *never* lie to you."

I wrapped my arms around him and held him against me. His warmth blanketed me. Gorm moved toward my mouth. He stopped mid-way and stared into my eyes.

"Why do you do that?"

He pushed my hair off my face. "I'm still amazed. You're so

beautiful and you don't even know it."

I smiled. "You're *so* good to me." I couldn't decide whether or not to look at his eyes or his lips.

He reached his hand behind my head and tilted my face toward him.

Lips. Definitely lips.

"You're worth it," he said.

I laughed. "Sometimes."

He grinned. "All the time."

Gorm pressed his lips and his body against me. He outsized me by a foot and at least a hundred pounds, but the difference didn't matter. He centered himself on me. I reached down, unbuttoned my shorts and unbuckled his belt. It released with a snap. I looked down between us and then up at him and smiled. *Thank you, Jesus.*

"And you always seem surprised."

"Well, it has only been *one* other time and I wanted to make sure, you know that it wasn't beginners luck."

Gorm howled. "No, it hasn't changed. It's still..."

"Enormous?"

His cheeks flushed.

I reached down and held him in my hand. "Wow. How great is that?"

"Pretty great," he said and raised himself off me to pull off his hoodie. He threw it on the floor. His chest was hairy in all the right places. Not too much, not too little. Perfect. He wrestled out of his jeans and returned between my legs.

He pulled off my shorts until they slid down to my ankle. I kicked off my flip-flops. They flung in the air and landed somewhere behind us. Gorm slipped off my panties.

Thank God I wore the good stuff today.

He tossed my lacy thong in the direction of his clothes.

I wrapped my bare, tanned legs around his waist. He dove into me and my back instinctively arched to meet him. *Yes. God, yes.* I couldn't talk. A low moan rose from my throat and enveloped us both.

Gorm buried his head in the nape of my neck. My tender skin came alive with pleasure. His unshaven face rubbed against my chin as the rush of our bodies collided on the cool ceramic.

My hands traveled the course of his body, pulling him deeper into me. His gruff voice pierced the silence, only making me crave him more.

"God, you're sexy."

My body spiked in pleasure. Gorm increased his rhythm to meet my fevered pitch. I dug my mouth into his shoulder. The muffled sound of my voice pleaded with him, "Don't stop. Please. Don't. Stop."

Sweat dropped from his forehead onto me. I dug my hands into his back, tightened my legs around his waist as my body constricted and grabbed hold of him.

The frenzied pace quickened until we peaked together. Our bodies contracted and released in unison. We collapsed in each other's arms. His scent and lips were all over me.

I closed my eyes and took a deep breath. I inhaled a mixture of his musky aftershave and spice-scented deodorant.

He kissed my neck and pulled me into a tight embrace. He dropped his head into the soft hollow between my neck and collarbone. I ran my fingers over his beautiful, bald head.

"Dani, I..."

I tried to slow down my breathing. "Me too, Gorm."

CHAPTER 25

"GOOD MORNING, learners!" I felt light on my feet and content in my heart. *Life is grand.* I smiled at the group that had assembled in their usual formation in the middle of the room.

"In classic Dickens' style we visited the past. Recollecting moments from our childhood and youth often remind us of a time of great innocence and equally great awakenings."

The murmur of agreement and head nods assured me I remained on the genealogical path they desired.

"As you've probably discovered from our in-class memory prompts and take-home writing assignments, the past will unearth people, places and influences that shaped who you are today."

Richard sat in the front row. He raised his finger as if to let me know he was present and accounted for.

I shot a wink in his direction. *Did I seriously just do that? Wow. Note to self: Do not teach after getting laid the day before.*

In the row behind Richard, Jean looked like she hadn't left the sixties. With her hair pulled back in a high ponytail, combined with the Peter Pan collar on her white blouse and her tan Capris and Keds tennis shoes she had aged beautifully and looked impeccable. Still, her eyes told another story.

I softly smiled at her. *Why is she so sad? Does she still miss Andrew? What about her husband, this Charles guy, he sounds like a great guy. I know her son is. Why so sad? Does Andrew haunt her?*

I looked at my father's copy of *"A Christmas Carol"* that was on my desk. Dickens' characters were always tragic. I felt a twinge in my heart.

Oh, my gosh. Jean's straight out of another Dickens' novel, "Great Expectations." She's Miss Havisham waiting for the groom that never shows. Okay, maybe that's a stretch. Still...I don't know...I wish I could make it right for her, but I wouldn't even know where to begin.

The rest of the class shifted in their seats. They were engaged and waiting for me to move them out of the past and onto the next lesson. *Older adult learners are eager little beavers that's for sure.*

"The whole premise of the spirits were to help Ebenezer Scrooge clear away any ghosts from his past to pave way for the Christmas Yet To Come."

I walked to the dry erase board and picked up a marker. I wrote, *Yet To Come* in red ink.

I then picked up the book. "Do you remember that the Ghost of Christmas Yet To Come hounds Ebenezer with horrible visions of his future if he doesn't change his ways? Dickens aptly called this foreshadowing the 'shadows of what may be'."

I set the book down on the corner of the desk.

"So our focus today is going to be on the Yet To Come moments still before us. Now you may be asking yourself, how does this relate to genealogy?"

Richard tipped his finger in the air. "I was thinking that

exact same thing."

His fellow classmates chuckled.

"Not to worry," I said with a smile. "It all weaves back to genealogy. When you're building your family tree, it's easy to fill in names, birthdays and anniversaries on the varying limbs." I paused. "The story, though, behind those names is what truly creates a family heirloom. The story you're going to know best, the story you want to make sure to record, is your own."

Suddenly I thought of my dad. *Who's going to record his story?*

"Ah, I see where you're going with this." The twinkle in Richard's eye almost made me cry.

Instead, I smiled. *How much does my father remember? Why haven't I done this with him?*

I cleared my throat. "Whether your past was positive, poor or pitiful, most often there was a pivotal moment that redefined, and possibly reshaped, your future."

In that moment I heard myself speak as if someone else were talking. I knew what had reshaped my future. It was staring me in the face every time I saw my father struggle to remember... where he left his glasses, his academic journal, or recently, where he left his car.

Dementia. I glanced at the linoleum floor. The white tiles with gray specks looked like someone had sprinkled confetti across the classroom.

"Miss Quinn?" Jean's Southern drawl pulled me out of my morbid reverie.

"I'm sorry...lost my train of thought there for a minute."

"Darlin', that happens to me *all* the time," Jean said and the room erupted in laughter.

What a lovely future-mother-in-law. I grinned at my whimsy.

"Alright," I said when the chuckling died down. "Everyone please get a piece of paper and pen."

I didn't have to wait long. The seniors were seasoned students by now and had their pens poised. *What a great group!*

"For our in-class memory prompt I want you to reflect and respond to the following two questions. I'll write them on the board and please take your time. Reflect, then respond."

I picked up the red pen and wrote in large letters so everyone could see.

How has your past shaped your future?

Who in your past had the most influence, good or bad, on who you are today?

I tore out of piece of paper from my notebook, sat down and started to answer my own questions.

CHAPTER 26

THE CLASSROOM was empty. On Fridays the campus cleared out early. I could see the near vacant parking lot from the windows that lined the south wall of my classroom.

As I packed my briefcase I felt someone staring at me. I turned toward the door.

"Oh my gosh, Richard! You scared me."

His face remained neutral.

"Did you forget something?" I looked in the center of the room where he sat. There was a blue notebook on the edge of the desk where Vivian sat, but Richard's desk was bare.

"No. My ride isn't here yet."

I nodded. *Huh.* It seemed odd, but after my father recently misplaced his car, nothing surprised me.

"So quite a story in the paper last week," he said and shut the door behind him. He took a seat in the front row.

I feigned ignorance. He could be talking about anything. "Which one was that?" I stuffed a file folder in between a notebook and a binder. My briefcase bulged. *There's no way I'm going to make Dickens' fit.*

Richard pointed his finger at me. "Oh, you're good." He smiled. "The front page piece about the bones and that ring."

"Oh, yeah." I looked at my father's copy of Dickens' still on my desk.

"It was a shame we had to lose such a valuable employee over that."

I glanced at Richard. "I'm sorry? What? What employee?"

"Bob Dorsey."

My heartbeat began to pick up in pace. "What about Bob?"

Richard again wagged his finger back and forth. "Oh, now, come on. Don't take me for a fool."

I nervously laughed. "I'm not. I'm not sure I know what you're talking about."

Richard slowly nodded.

I looked for my cell phone. It was face down on my desk, but it was within reach. *Don't make it look obvious.* "So who's late picking you up today?" I casually leaned on my desk and reached for my phone.

"The cell reception is horrible in here," Richard said. "In fact, it's altogether non-existent."

I lightly chuckled. "Yeah, it can be trying at times, but if you'd like to call someone." I held the phone, but didn't extend it toward him.

"No thanks." Richard fanned away my nonexistent offer. "The call won't go through."

I pressed the side of my phone with my thumb to wake it up.

"I had Bob cut the wireless access, disconnect the telephone lines and the cell tower feed to this building before I fired him."

I laughed. "Sure, okay." I gave the A-OK signal with my hand. "Richard, you really had me going there for a second."

He glared at me. "It's not a joke."

Calm. I made my breathing slow down. *Stay calm. He*

doesn't know Bob. He's a crazy old man.

Richard slowly moved his head from side to side. The sound of *tsk, tsk* eerily rose from his throat. "It's a shame I had to cut Bob from the payroll." His eyes narrowed in on mine.

"I don't understand?" The screen on my cell phone burst red as it resumed life. A bar across the top reported what systems were functioning...none. *My phone just needs time to wake up.*

"Bill Hull's my son-in-law. Hellauva good guy."

"Ohhh-kay...I still don't understand what Bill has to do with Bob?"

Richard mocked a laugh. "Dani, Dani, Dani. Bill's the foreman for Birdseye Construction. He inherited the business when he married my daughter just like I inherited Hawkeye Construction when I married my wife. Bill is my *family*."

I nodded. *Crazy man what the hell does this have to do with me?*

"It's really unfair what Bob and Viv's son did to Bill in that story."

"What do you mean? Gorm didn't do anything, but report the facts."

Richard shook his finger at me. "Oh, you see there, that's where you're wrong. He reported half-truths, but I really shouldn't be surprised. The little bastard's just like his father."

"What? What are you talking about?"

Richard chuckled. "Oh, Charles Gorham's a good man, better than most. I wouldn't have married a woman that was knocked up with someone else's child."

"What the *hell* are you talking about?"

"Viv. She was damaged goods. Andrew soiled her. If I couldn't have her, then he sure as hell wasn't."

Enough of this shit. I looked at my cell phone. It was fully charged and active. A single bar showed it across the screen. I pressed the keypad and started dialing Gorm's number. I held it up to my ear. It started to ring. *Thank you God.* I sighed in relief. Then the call dropped. *What?* I held the phone out and tried again. *Please work. Please get a signal. Gorm, come find me. I tried to send Gorm a telepathic message.*

Richard remained sitting at his desk in the front row. A snide smile crossed his face. "I told you. Bob's last order of business was to cut Internet, Wi-Fi and cell tower access."

I started toward the door. I kept my focus on it as I made my way to the exit. I didn't look at Richard. I didn't want to see him so I was caught off guard by his leg. He must have extended it as I passed because I tripped right over it. I fell to the floor and dropped my phone when my body collided against the hard surface. My phone split apart. *Shit.* The battery skidded across the linoleum and the screen lay face up in front of me. It was black. *Damn it.*

Suddenly Richard was above me.

I looked up at him. *Oh dear God...please don't hurt me.* I couldn't settle down my breathing. Adrenaline shot through my body like rapid fire. My thoughts were equally as sporadic. *He's going to hurt me. Kick him in the groin. Scoot back and kick up.*

Richard leaned over me as if he was reading my mind to block a blow. "Did you know," he said in an even, unnerving tone, "that in the late seventeen hundreds when President Adams released the correspondence from our failed war negotiations with France that he replaced the names of the French intermediaries with the letters *W*, X, Y, and Z?"

I shook my head. *I need to get outta here.* Panic seized my chest. *Screw this guy and his crazy rant.*

Richard extended his hand. "Please, Miss Quinn, this won't take long if you'd just listen to me."

Calm. Cool. Collected. I reluctantly grabbed his hand. He

pulled me to my feet.

"Please," he extended his arm toward the classroom, "sit down."

I shook my head. I backed away from him until my ass pressed against the edge of my desk. Bells and whistles continued to sound that I needed to make a run for it, but how?

"Suit yourself." Richard sat back at his desk.

I gently pressed against the back of my desk and tried to create more distance between psycho and me, but it was too heavy. The desk wouldn't move. *Shit*.

"Most historians," he continued, "only focus on the three French diplomats who tried to convince the Americans to pay a bribe to discuss war negotiations. Their identities were hidden by the letters X, Y, and Z in Adams' report that he released to the press."

Richard slapped his hands together. I flinched.

"You see there," he said, "sometimes the press can be used for good." Richard shook his head. "But," he rigidly held up his finger, "there was a fourth man, an Englishman who worked for a Dutch bank the Americans used. He was the initial point of contact for the war negotiations. He was identified as W. But no one seems to remember him." Richard's voice and focus seemed to trail off. "No one remembers W."

"Well, you do." I kept the tone of my voice even and soft. I tried to show interest in his ramblings.

Richard seemed to take it as his cue. His voice gained momentum. "W, though, was key. The Americans wouldn't have been put in contact with X, Y, and Z if it weren't for W." He slammed the palm of his hand on the desk.

Startled, I pressed against the desk. The corner bit into my lower back. I glanced at the two pieces of my phone on the floor. I smiled at Richard and gently knelt down without ever losing eye contact with him. I reached for one half of my phone when he again smacked his hand against his desk.

"Your phone's not important right now. This is!" He slapped his hand on his desk for what appeared to be my final warning. "Pay attention!" His voice was loud and insistent.

I shot up off the ground. My phone remained scattered in pieces on the floor. *Do I have any weapons?* I looked at my briefcase and the Dickens' book. A ballpoint pen, attached to a file folder, stuck out of the top of my briefcase. *If I can grab it, I can stab the freak with it.*

"Don't you see?"

I looked back at Richard. *Crap.*

"W was a valuable part of the negotiations. He put the entire event in motion."

"Huh." My voice shook. I cleared my throat to compose myself. "I did *not* know that."

"Of course you didn't! Your father probably fed you lies about the entire event."

I said nothing.

"Nicholas Hubbard."

"I'm sorry?" I shook my head. "Richard, I don't know who that is."

"Of course you don't! He was the Englishman that worked for the Dutch bank. He was the W in the published papers. *No one* knows the W or that there was even a W. But let me tell you," Richard's finger pointed toward me. Even though I knew he couldn't reach me from where he sat, I still reacted by leaning back. I practically arched against the desk.

"If it wasn't for W there wouldn't have been an X, Y, or Z," he said.

I nodded. *Maybe if I let him tell this story I can leave nicely.*

He turned his finger toward himself and jabbed it into his

chest. "I'm W. I put the entire X, Y, Z group together. I did!"

I remembered the photo my mom had taken of the X, Y, Z Affair banquet. The one man at my father's table without a ring had a thin face and faint mustache. I looked at Richard. His face was hollow and his mustache remained a shadow of hair above his top lip. *Oh my hell. It's Richard. He was the creepy guy mom talked about.*

"*I* put the fraternity all together," he said. "I talked to your father and Andrew about it and then they turned on me. They stole the idea right out from underneath me and started their own little group. Then they had the gall to keep me out of it!" Richard glared at me. "You're just like him, *aren't you?*"

"What?" I moved closer to my briefcase and the copy of Dickens. The pen was a crapshoot, but I could easily grab the book. "What are you talking about?"

"Oh, I think you know." Richard reached into his back pant pocket.

I stiffened. My heart raced and my hands started to sweat.

He flung something at me. My hands quickly rose to shield my face. A folded newspaper article landed on my desk.

"I thought you were smarter than this," he said.

I glanced at the dateline. It was a week old. Gorm's name appeared above the fold. *Oh God.* It was the story about the bones.

"I told you to stop digging where you didn't belong, but I guess..." He shook his head and got up from his desk. He slowly drew closer to me. With each creepy step the ringing in my ears got louder. *Run!*

"Richard!" I yelled. "Back off." I held my hand out in front of me. "I don't know what's going on, but you need to leave – now." I pointed toward the door. "Get out of my classroom, now!"

He flashed a sinister smile. His eyes darkened and narrowed.

There was no twinkle or shine, only foreboding.

"All bite and no bark. I guess you're more like your father than I knew. He always talked a great game...but in the end, he was no better off than I was." He grinned. "He didn't get her and neither did I."

Vivian. I ran around my desk and sprinted toward the door. Richard grabbed me just as I reached for the handle. *Old man moves fast. Shit.*

I screamed. "Let go!" I jerked my arm and kicked. His hold on me was too great. He twisted my arm behind my back. I winced in pain. "Let me go!" He pressed me up against the door and cranked my arm behind me to a near breaking point.

"You're as easy as he was." Richard's breath was on my neck. Shivers ran down my spine.

"Get away from me!" I squirmed, but he only tightened his grip.

"I didn't expect it to be that simple," he hissed in my ear, "but it was. It was almost too easy."

Richard yanked my arm up behind me until I started to cry.

"*Please* this has nothing to do with me. Let me go." My back was toward him. I stared at the door. Safety was just beyond its reach.

Suddenly the door handle started to twist from the outside. "Help!" I screamed. "Help!"

Richard strengthened his hold on me. "Shut up." His voice cut through my eardrum.

Again, I kicked my leg back toward him but I swung at air. "Help!"

Richard put his other hand over my mouth. I tried to bite him.

The door handle kept twisting. "Miss Quinn?" Her Southern accent seeped beneath the door. "Are you alright?"

It's now or never. I shook my head. "Vivian!" I screamed into Richard's hand. He shoved me hard against the door. I slammed into it. "Vivian! Help!" I wiggled and moved so that I was hard to hold. With my free hand, I fumbled with the doorknob. The lock unclicked. Richard lost his hold on me. I twisted the doorknob and it flung open, practically knocking Vivian over.

I pushed her back into the hallway. "Run!"

"No," she said evenly. "You go." She pointed toward the exit. "Get help."

I shook my head. "No, you've got to go. He's crazy!" I grabbed her arm. She held her hand over mine. "It's okay. Go get help."

Richard backed up into the classroom as Vivian walked inside.

"Viv." Richard stood by my desk.

"Richard," she spoke sharply, "what have you done?"

I stood in the doorway unable to move. *What the hell is she doing?* I was paralyzed. *What do I do? Who do I call? Where is a phone?*

"I was trying to protect you," he said. His eyes changed in intensity. They filled with deep emotion.

"From what? What were you doing to Miss Quinn?"

"You don't understand." He pointed toward me. I took a step back into the safe distance of the hallway.

"She threatened to ruin everything." He grabbed the newspaper off my desk. "This! This garbage." He seethed and moved toward Vivian. "She got your little bastard to help her."

Vivian gasped.

"You didn't think I knew about that?" Richard's eyes darkened. "Your *bastard* son."

Vivian pulled her hand back and came forward with it across Richard's cheek. The contact was hard and loud. Richard touched his face.

"Why would you do that?" Stunned he backed away from her. "I love you. I've always loved you. That's why...I did what I did."

"What did you do?" She moved toward him. "What did you do? How do you know about Christopher?"

"You told me." Richard's eyes looked wounded.

"There are only three people who know the truth about Christopher's paternity and you aren't one of them."

"Viv, that evening at the XYZ Affair, I was sitting beside you when you said you were pregnant."

Oh holy hell. She was pregnant?

"No," Vivian shook her head. "I told Andrew that I was carrying his child. I never *ever* spoke to you." She held her hand over her mouth. "Oh, my God! What did you do? Where's Andrew?"

"Viv, he soiled you."

Vivian gasped. "No, Andrew loved me. We loved each other. We were going to get married."

Richard shook his finger at her. "No, that was never going to happen."

"Richard, what did you *do*?"

He stepped toward her and reached out to touch her. She recoiled from him. "Leave me alone. Get. Away."

"You don't understand. Andrew wasn't good enough for you."

"Andrew was all I ever wanted."

Richard chortled. "No, that's just the lie he made you believe. He admitted he didn't really love you."

"No," she shook her head. "Andrew would never have said that."

"Oh, but he did." Richard grinned. "When I led him to the roof of this old building." Richard pointed his finger toward the ceiling. "Andrew *swore* he'd leave town. Of course, I knew it was a lie. But then he said he didn't want you. That he was through with you." Richard slowly moved his head back and forth. "I couldn't allow that."

Vivian moved toward Richard and grabbed a fistful of his shirt. "What did you do?"

"What W should have done years ago. I regained my place in society. I took charge. I rid myself *and* you of the roadblock that was between us."

Vivian hit her fist against his chest. "What did you do?"

"What any gentleman seeking peace would do. I offered Andrew the choice between you or freedom. He chose wrong and had to pay the penalty. I didn't mean for him to die. I just wanted to send a warning. But...it was spring and the roof was slick with moisture." Richard shrugged. "Accidents happen all the time on a construction site." A smile of yellowing teeth filled his face.

It was like a one-two punch to the stomach. *He killed Andrew. The bones. Oh my God!* I took a deep breath as all the pieces fit together. *That was Gorm's father.*

Vivian dropped to her knees. "No. No. No." She covered her face with her hands.

I ran toward her and knelt down beside her. I placed my hand on her back.

Richard looked down at her and then at me.

I clenched my hand into a fist. Richard shook his head before he walked past us and out the door.

CHAPTER 27

IT DIDN'T take Campus Security long to locate Richard. He was in one of the on-site construction trailers drinking a beer. They escorted him to the police department for questioning.

Vivian and I were still in the classroom answering a police investigator's questions when Gorm ran into the room. My heartbeat quickened. I needed Gorm and a hot bath...maybe even together.

"Mom, are you alright?" He looked at her.

Then he looked at me.

"Oh my God! Dani."

The start of two black eyes and a swollen nose from landing face first on the floor was the eyeful he got. He ran his hands over his bald head. His face was a map of pain.

He turned back to his mom.

"Is it true? Dani's father told me that...the bones...that... they're..."

Vivian stood up and wrapped her arms around her son. "I'm sorry." She looked small beside her son.

Gorm leaned over to bury his head on his mom's shoulder.

"No. I never got to meet him."

Tears fell down my cheeks.

"He's been this secret my whole life," Gorm said.

His mother nodded and rubbed his back. "Christopher, I'm sorry. I was trying to protect you."

"From what?" Gorm pulled away from her. His eyes sparked with anger.

"From this. I knew your father would never just leave me. His disappearance has always troubled me. Andrew wouldn't just leave...not when he knew I was pregnant."

"But you could have told me his name. I deserved to know the name of my biological father."

Vivian gently touched his cheek. "I'm sorry. I thought I was doing what was best for you."

Gorm's jaw clenched. "All that did was create an indefinable hole in my life."

I watched Vivian lovingly look into her son's eyes. "Andrew. Petrov. Your father's name is Andrew Petrov."

Suddenly, I smiled. The strong features, the solid build, his stubborn, persistent nature. *Ahh, he's Russian.*

Gorm looked over at me. His sapphire-colored eyes were glassy. They brimmed on the verge of tears.

"I'm sorry," was all I could say.

He nodded. "Me too." He wiped his eyes with his palm and put his hand on his hip.

He's trying so hard to keep it together.

He cleared his throat. "From what your dad told me..." Gorm paused and lowered his head for a moment.

I felt my heart sink to my stomach. *What can I do to make this better for him?*

He glanced up and looked at me. I held him with my eyes.

"Well, it sounds like this Andrew was a pretty standup guy," he said.

I tilted my head. "Oh..." My voice cracked with emotion. "That doesn't surprise me at all." I swallowed the lump in my throat. "Considering what I know about his son."

Gorm shook his head. "Oh, man. I wish..." He rubbed his chin. "I wish I could've known him."

His mother softly cried beside him. "I do, too."

CHAPTER 28

My FATHER quietly walked into my classroom. He had the shadow of a beard and the day old scruff looked good on the old man. I looked up at him from my desk.

"Daniella," he said. Tears began to instantly stream down his face. "You're hurt.'"

I shook my head. "I'm okay. I think it looks worse than it is."

"I'm sorry," he said, rubbing his forehead.

The worry on his face and the concern in his eyes was a balm all their own.

"I should've paid more attention to you and worried less about my damn reputation." He gently moved hair away from my face and kissed my forehead. His voice lowered to a whisper. "Are you okay? Be honest."

"I am." I tilted my head toward Gorm, who stood beside his mother. "But he isn't." I started to cry. "Dad...please do something, say something. Make it better."

My father nodded and walked over to Gorm, whose face was riddled with sorrow. My dad reached into the pocket of his pants and withdrew a ring.

"When your father and I decided to form our own fraternity, Andrew wanted to solidify the union, the brotherhood. That's the kind of man your father was. He believed in a code of honor where a man's promise was his covenant."

My father looked at the ring in his hand. It suddenly seemed small in the palm. "This ring is part of that promise. It's been a gentle reminder all these years to be honest, forthright and compassionate."

Dad turned toward me. "I've somewhat failed in the latter category." He looked back at Gorm, "I know you won't. You have all the same qualities as your father. You're a good man. I know your father would be proud." He held the ring out to Gorm.

"Was that my dad's?" Gorm's voice was barely above a whisper.

My father softly smiled. "No. Apparently my pull on campus isn't as great as I'd like to believe." He started to laugh. "The county coroner has your father's remains and his ring. Both will be returned to you when the investigation concludes. I didn't want you to have to wait to have an important piece of your past. Your father would want you to be part of our brotherhood."

Gorm nodded. "Thank you." He slid the ring on his right ring finger and looked at his hand with solemn reverence.

CHAPTER 29

I STEPPED on the newspaper when I opened the front door to retrieve it. Gorm's house was in the distance. I scooped the paper off the porch and felt the sun kiss the top of my head.

I glanced at the headline: *Identity of Bones Found at Cowboy University Unearthed* the caption beneath the story read, *Local man arrested, pending trial.*

I stepped inside and was about to bump the front door closed with my hip when I flipped the paper over and saw Gorm's byline below the fold. I leaned against the doorframe and started reading.

The Search is Over
By Chris Gorham, Times Staff Writer

Casper, WY – I was warned by well-intentioned friends that searching for my biological father would only end in disaster.

What my friends couldn't possibly have known was that the one thing my biological father could do for me, at age 47, was to fill the void and ease the emptiness I carried daily since I discovered I wasn't related to the man who raised me.

In a word, I wanted closure.

Closure came at a cost when I later realized that the bones, discovered at Cowboy State University, which I handled, photographed and wrote about, were the bones of my father.

Perhaps it's the reason I was so drawn to uncovering the identity of the skeletal remains that were buried and left to rot beside a cement bag 47 years ago. Or perhaps it was the harsh reality that no one seemed to care that bothered me most.

I looked across the green belt that separated my parents' house and Gorm's. Dew clung to the top of the grass. I was barefoot and in a pair of sweats. I touched my hair as if I could make out its disheveled appearance simply by feeling it. And I could. *I'm a scary mess.*

I stared at his house and then back at his column.

New friends, like Bob Dorsey, the maintenance worker at Cowboy State University who first unearthed my father's remains and later risked his career to help me break the story, unknowingly become integral in this journey of self-discovery.

In fact, Richard Albright, retired chief operating officer and primary stakeholder in Hawkeye Construction, fired Dorsey. Albright fired Dorsey without cause. However, Dorsey was reinstated to his position both with Hawkeye Construction and Cowboy State University when details of Albright's involvement with concealing a death became known.

Albright married Beverly Hawkeye, in the summer

of 1965. As part of her dowry, Richard was given stock and a management position with the family-run business, Hawkeye Construction.

Albright grew the company by securing state-funded construction projects below bid and hiring state employees below cost. Hawkeye Construction led to the development of Birdseye Construction, which Albright entrusted with his son-in-law, Bill Hull.

Hull was the foreman on duty when Dorsey discovered the human remains. Hull literally shelved the bones in a gunnysack per instructions from Albright and considered the matter closed.

Albright was arrested and charged this week with manslaughter for the death of my father, Andrew Petrov.

On the evening of Saturday, April 17, 1964 my mother and father were attending The XYZ Affair, in honor of the University's political science department. It was on that night that my mother revealed to my father that she was pregnant. With plans to elope to Las Vegas and live off-campus while they finished their degrees, their future looked bright. However, when my father left to pack a change of clothes for their trip, he never returned.

My mom was left pregnant, heartbroken and searching for the answer as to why my father suddenly vanished from her life.

According to police records, Albright allegedly intercepted my father and led him to the roof of the former Administrative Building with the alleged pretense of needing help to look for a water leak.

A struggle ensued and my father supposedly fell to

his death.

According to city building permits, the University's last expansion project began in the spring of 1964. Hawkeye Construction, the parent company of Birdseye, was the company on record. Albright allegedly buried my father and was involved in his death.

A court will ultimately decide Albright's involvement and culpability.

So where does that leave a bastard son?

I shook my head, but the word remained in print. *Did he just refer to himself as a bastard? Oh my gosh.* I held the paper closer and reread it. *Why would he do that?*

"You must have gotten to the part about being a bastard."

I jumped. "Son of a—"

Gorm stood at the base of the steps leading to my parents' house. *This is how I first met you.* His cowboy hat shaded his blue eyes, but it didn't stop them from twinkling.

"Hi." My stomach fluttered.

A crooked smile filled his face. "Hi to you, too."

Gorm slowly walked up the steps and made his way toward me. He peeked over the paper. "Yup, you're at the bastard part."

"How did you...what makes you think that?"

"The look on your face. Dani, you should *never* play poker."

I chuckled. "I just don't understand why you would call yourself a bastard."

Gorm shrugged. "When you're the product of an illegitimate birth and your father's identity is unknown, bastard kinda fits."

"Technically, but is that how you really see yourself?"

Gorm nudged his head toward the paper. "Finish the story. It's a Pulitzer Prize winning piece."

I smiled widely before resuming my place in his column.

For this bastard son, I lived with a hole inside me,

which is like living with a secret. You get up and go to work, laugh at work, and act like everything is fine. But you know that in your life, there's something missing and you're never fulfilled.

Until the blanks can be filled in, my family tree has only started with me and extended to my sons. The branches above me have been barren—until now.

Now, I have the name and more importantly the identity of my father. Andrew Petrov believed in commitment and lived by a code of honor that exceeded any image I had of who my father was or what he represented.

In the end, finding my father allowed me to find myself.

My throat tightened and my eyes moistened.

"Chris." It was the first time I had ever called him by his name. I reached out and placed my hand on his heart. "This is the most beautiful piece I have ever read...bar none."

He softly smiled. "Really?"

I nodded. "Oh, yeah. It's amazing. You," I said with my hand firmly on his chest, "are amazing."

Gorm placed his hand over mine. "I wouldn't have found my dad or, really, myself if it hadn't been for you."

I shook my head. "No, that's not true."

He held my hand tightly against him. "Dani, since the moment I met you, I knew you were different."

I playfully bobbed my head from side to side. "Well, there's something every girl wants to hear."

"No, that's not what I meant." He softly smiled at me. "Dani, you're different because despite everything that's happened, you're still open and willing to risk. You haven't let your past shape your future. If anything you defy it. You made me want to move forward and then," he pulled me closer toward him, "you made it happen that I could."

My tears fell onto our hands. "I *really* like you," I said.

Gorm squeezed my hand, "I passed 'like' a long time ago. Dani, I love you."

I couldn't respond. *Really?* My heart was in my throat. *You love me?*

Gorm gently kissed me and then whispered in my ear. "Forever and ever."

CHAPTER 30

HOME

MY MOM took a step back from the picnic table and appraised her work. A bright red, rugged bandanna-print table runner flowed down the center of the cherry wood tabletop. Simple white plates and blue serving bowls added a patriotic splash to the table setting. A glass pitcher of fresh lemonade seemed to wave away the summer heat. It was going to be a good old-fashioned western barbeque.

"I think we've got everything we need and if we don't..." She swatted a fly with her dishtowel. "Then the hell with it."

I smiled and tilted my head. "Mom, it's *perfect*. Thank you."

"For what?"

"For doing this."

"Oh, *this* is nothing." She kissed my forehead. "Wait until your wedding."

I started to laugh. "Yeah, well, we're both going to have to wait...I don't see that happening...Oh my gosh! They're here!"

The green Jeep pulled into my parents' driveway. My stomach fluttered as butterflies took flight. Gorm stepped out of his Jeep. I could see his smile from where I stood. He opened the rear door of his Jeep. His mother and stepfather emerged hand-in-hand.

I turned toward my mom. "Can you believe it?" I asked.

Mom was distracted. She watched my father make his way toward her. Her face filled with joy. He reached for her hand and stood beside her at the head of the table. They looked at me and then at Gorm.

"What are you waiting for?" my father asked.

I hurried to meet him.

Home. If home had a feeling it was the warmth and security I felt whenever I held hands with Gorm. He took my hand and I stared into his clear blue eyes.

When I looked at him, I didn't see who I wanted to be in his eyes, I saw who I was. A woman that had moved halfway across the state to return home, in order to start over.

ACKNOWLEDGMENTS

WRITING IS all I know. So I am extremely fortunate to have a network that supports me and serves as a safety net when I feel like I'm falling in my craft. These are the people that have touched my life and forever changed it.

John Koehler – Who knew that an unintended email response would lead to such a fun publishing union? Thank you for welcoming me into the Koehler family. You are a king amongst men and the kindest man in this industry.

Joe Coccaro – To my editor at Koehler Books who made me first believe in this story when you told me that my work deserved to be published. And added that you wanted this book. Joe - you had me at published. Thank you for wanting this book and preserving my voice through the editing process. I hope we can work together again.

Ruth Putnam – My Ruth. You were my very first friend in Casper. From your pocket-pants to your knowledge of all things computer-related, you bring humor and depth to my life. You are a surrogate mom, sister and friend. Where would I be without you? Thank you for allowing me to bring our friendship into this story. We really are this fun.

Gayle Schnorenberg – From brainstorming story ideas on napkins at lunch – you kept me sane throughout this process. And fed! Thank you for believing in me.

Ben Schanck – Who knew that a history assignment for my twin boys would lead to a novel? Learning about the history of The XYZ Affair made this story come to life. You are an educator any teacher would admire. And I certainly do.

Terri Stepp – Did you think I would forget you? Every year, you send me a calendar for Christmas. That calendar keeps me on track so that I can juggle kids, classes and writing. We have been friends for a very long time and we always will.

Dana Volney – You taught me to look for silver linings and in doing so you reawakened my love of this craft. How do I ever thank you for that gift? You were my beta reader, editor and cheerleader for this story. In your light, I never doubt myself. You are a forever friend.

To Jackie Willhite at Beauty Grafix who kept me blonde during this process. Dusti Barker – who kept my writing hands in shape. And to Kimberly Taylor – a brilliant photographer because you capture the true spirit of a person. You made it fun. Thank you.

To all my fellow learners in the Master of Arts in Adult and Post-Secondary Education program at the University of Wyoming – Class of 2014 – Hoorah! In it. To win it. We did it! I am a better adult educator and writer because of each of you. Thank you for enriching my life.

To my little brother – Patrick Flanagan Billiter. From the moment mom brought you home from the hospital, I considered you mine. Ours is a bond like no other. I simply adore you.

To my brother Stephen Billiter, who is a tough editor, but makes me a stronger writer. I love you Tbone.

And my sister Suzanne Billiter Cragin – You are my first call. When life is good or hard, yours is the voice I want to hear. When I need to laugh, you always provide a funny story that makes me realize the Billiter women are just klutzy! Cute, but klutzy. I love you more than you will ever know.

Finally to the most important people in my life – my children – Austin, Kyle, Ciara and Cooper. God richly blessed me with each of you.

Austin, your humor and smile bring light to our home. You are a natural leader. I'd follow you anywhere.

Kyle, my sweet son, you know me better than anyone. You understand and protect the tenderhearted. I know you're destined for greatness.

Ciara. My little girl. My answered prayer. Your strength and courage awe me. Your heart inspires me.

And my little boy, Cooper James. You are a writer's dream and a mother's blessing. You draw beautiful pictures and take me inside a world where hope lives and love never hurts.

My children – Thank you for going on this crazy adventure with me. I love you with everything I have and all that I am.